SECTORS

by

Brick Marlin

Bill Marl

WHISKEY CREEK PRESS

www.whiskeycreekpress.com

"Thanks for your support!"

Published by
WHISKEY CREEK PRESS

Whiskey Creek Press
PO Box 51052
Casper, WY 82605-1052
www.whiskeycreekpress.com

ISBN 978-1-61160-359-0

Credits
Cover Artist: Kendra Egert
Editor: Stephanie Parent
Printed in the United States of America

Dedication

~~This book is dedicated to you, Dear Reader. May you have your laughs, your thrills, and your dark fears fuse together as you enter the Sectors.~~

Chapter 1

Walking through the dark in the abandoned house, Gilbert shuddered. Thoughts twirling inside his head of being in this abandoned old house that had been condemned over fifty years ago were frightening enough for a young boy such as him. And being inside the walls of the house was, well, downright scary—but, at the same time, fun!

There was a large red sign out front that strictly stated: *KEEP OUT! NO TRESPASSING! VIOLATERS WILL BE FINED A MINIMUM OF $500 OR PLACED IN JAIL!* Gilbert felt adventurous, ignoring the warning sign, wondering: Could the cops possibly fine an eleven-year-old boy that much money, or place him in jail?

Gilbert didn't think so—or at least he hoped not. Although his mind did give him a dreadful picture of being in jail with another guy who smelled like rotten eggs and had onion-breath whenever he spoke. Some guy who had been in jail for murder, robbery, and tearing off the heads of troll dolls just because of the multicolored hair.

That thought didn't set well in his gut. But he figured with the help of his comrade in arms, he felt pretty doggone safe. He would not have to worry about sharing a cell with a smelly dude.

"You know that over a hundred people died in this house back in the Civil War days?" a voice spoke behind Gilbert's ear.

"Bobby, I know that isn't true because the place wasn't even built back then."

"How do you know?" Bobby's flashlight speared the dark, revealing the vulgar graffiti on the walls.

"Because my mom told me so."

"What, does she know everything?" Bobby's flashlight caught a huge gash in the wall, and he wondered if someone had taken a sledge hammer to it.

"She knows you like her homemade Mexican pizzas on Fridays after school," he told Bobby, "so you'd better can it!"

Not much of a response came from the peanut gallery, except: "Well, ya got me there, Gilbert."

Gilbert and Bobby could not be separated if the ground split open between them. One boy would simply take the chance and leap to the other, while the other would reach out with both hands and catch him. That was true friendship. Best friends for life. End of story. They had only been good friends—I mean *best* friends—three years running. Ever since the day Gilbert saw Bobby and his parents move into the house two doors down.

And on that particular day, under a bright orange orb that hung in the sky, radiating enough heat and humidity for the residents of Deputy Point, causing them to turn down their thermostats to allow the cold air to drift through the vents like an apparition floating through a wall, Gilbert saw Bobby bring out his bike—a cool silver and black BMX with mag wheels and a plastic racing plate tied onto the handlebars that displayed the number one.

The magnificent sight of his bicycle filled Gilbert's eyes, making him a bit envious. He went into the garage and got his out. Unfortunately it wasn't as neat as Bobby's, being pieced together from other bike parts, but it did suffice. After a brief introduction between the two boys, finding out a few things they had in common, such as what kind of movies they liked and how much they hated—and I do mean *hated*—liver and onions, they took off together and rode down to the end of street and into the woods through the bike trails that delivered them above and beyond. And along the way they found they had even more things in common, too.

It sparked an instant friendship.

So, now, together with Bobby's little brother Timmy tagging along because if he didn't he would run and tell his mom they were going into the abandoned house down by the river, they slowly traipsed through the abandoned house.

"Are you sure your mom isn't going to be home until ten, Bobby?"

"I told you already. She works until nine thirty. And, I just got a cell phone. So if she does happen to call, I'll just say we're outside in the tent."

Gilbert had told his parents he was staying the night at Bobby's. What his parents didn't know was that he and Bobby were going into the old house, which they had strongly forbidden him to do for years. But he was a kid, full of energy, and very curious about the house. Every time he and his parents would drive by it, he would ask if the place had a history. And every time there was a long pause before his father would reply with, "Gilbert," then a short pause while his father formed the right words in his brain to say, "Don't let either your mother or me catch you in there. You understand, son?"

Gilbert would sigh, replying, "Yeah."

Then they would say, "Good. Because young boys with curious minds, like you, do not need to be in that house."

"Promise me you won't go in there," Mom demanded.

Crossing his fingers and hiding his hand behind his back, Gilbert replied with a grin, "Sure, Mom."

A cold breeze blew through the old house, and Gilbert could have sworn he heard something move behind them. He thought he heard a…was that a moan? Training his flashlight's beam on the empty hallway they had just exited, he found nothing in sight.

"Hear something, Gilbert?" Timmy asked.

"I thought I did. Coulda sworn I did."

"Probably nothing," Bobby informed him. "I'm not sure if I believe in ghosts or not."

"I do!" Timmy's voice was loud.

"Timmy, you'd believe in anything."

"Nu-uh!"

"Oh, I remember when you thought you saw Bigfoot out

in our woods last summer. You ran and told Mom it was out there."

"I thought it was. Really!"

"Remember that, Gilbert?"

"Think so." After a short pause, while allowing the memory to seep back into his brain: "Who *was* that out there, anyway?"

"Skeleton man. Mr. Stiles. That weird old man who lives on the other side of the woods."

Gilbert pondered on it for a bit, the picture of Mr. Stiles' thin frame in his mind, the skin very taut around his bones. "That's right! I had forgotten about that guy. Some say he lives in the woods."

"No telling," Bobby replied as his beam splashed the stairs to go down to the second level. "All I know is that guy gives me the creeps!"

"Me too!" Timmy added.

Bobby smiled. "Timmy, you are afraid of your own shadow."

Timmy's red Popsicle face scowled.

Gilbert brought up the rear and heard something behind him again. He looked over his shoulder, not training his light on it this time, and could have sworn he saw a shadow move in front of an open door where the moon shone through. He blinked and it was gone.

His stomach tightened, and he stopped.

Bobby had his foot on the first step to descend, glanced back, and asked, "You okay, Gilbert?"

For a moment Gilbert didn't respond; then he said, "Yeah. I'm fine. Thought I saw something. Now it's gone."

Timmy stepped beside Gilbert. "See a ghost, Gilbert?"

"I don't know what it was."

"Well, I believe in 'em," he boasted.

"Like I said," Bobby added, "you'll believe in *any*thing, Timmy."

After the sound of Timmy's huffing, the three descended the steps, one by one, until they stood in front of a window on the second floor. A river reflected back through the glass.

"You all ready to go? Bobby asked. "We've already been through the entire place."

Gilbert and Timmy agreed and followed Bobby down to the first floor and out the door. In their wake a white face appeared on the windowpane. Seconds later there was the sound of racing footsteps slipping outside, right before the front door latched shut.

* * * *

Bobby's mom came home around ten 'o clock. Gilbert, Timmy, and Bobby were in the midst of a role-playing game under a tent set up in the backyard.

"Hey! That ain't right! How come I got shot?"

"Timmy, you chose to step out into the hallway and try to see what was out there. Gilbert's character tried to tell you not to. But you did anyway. And it didn't help that you rolled a two on the dice, not giving you much of a chance."

"But I only have ten Life Points left!"

"Well, since you were hit by a laser cannon called a Turmoil, I wouldn't have to wonder why."

Timmy huffed, crossed his arms. "Stupid gun! Still isn't fair that I don't have one!"

"You didn't have enough cash back at the scene in the alley where we bought our stuff from that dark man," Gilbert said.

"Yeah," Bobby explained, "you could have bought a gun instead of a sword."

"But I wanted to be able to creep up on the guards and slice 'em up like a samurai warrior!"

"Not when they have a Turmoil," Bobby defended. "That is the beast of all the weapons." He glanced at Gilbert. "Right, man?"

"Yep. That's why I've got one." Gilbert beamed, piecing together a picture of a rifle in his mind with a thick barrel that swiveled like a Gatlin gun, shooting both ice and fire bullets. "My turn, isn't it?"

"Yeah," Bobby said. "What do you want to do?"

"I'll roll the dice and see if I can counterattack whoever's in the hall."

"Cool."

Gilbert rolled the twelve-sided die, and it gave him a ten. He smiled. "I'll take out my Turmoil and peek around the corner."

"You're safe. The guy doesn't see you," Bobby said. "Roll again if you want to try and shoot the guy. See if you hit him."

Timmy scowled and mumbled something under his breath while Gilbert rolled a twelve.

"Dang! You killed the dude!" Bobby said. "Splattered his brains all over the walls and floor!"

"Cool!" Gilbert replied as he and Bobby high-fived each other. He looked at Timmy, who sat there pouting. "Saved your life, man. Now you can use one of your Med Patches and cover that wound."

"It'll add thirty Life Points to your character," Bobby said.

"So? This game is stupid!"

"Well, don't play it," Bobby said defensively.

"I won't! I wanted to kill that guy and get a bunch of points. It ain't fair!" Timmy stood up and ran out of the tent.

Bobby and Gilbert watched him go and glanced at each other.

"Kids," Bobby said, shaking his head.

"Kids," Gilbert agreed.

Then they both chuckled.

"Sorry, bro," Bobby said.

"No problem," Gilbert replied.

"You know how Timmy is." Bobby shook his head again, grinning.

Still chuckling, Gilbert said, "I know, man. No sweat. Hey, I gotta go pee. Drank way too much Coke."

"Go over there by the woods if you wanna, instead of going into the house."

Gilbert pondered it. "Might just do that. Timmy might be in there or something."

"If he is, he's crying his eyes out." Bobby snickered.

As Gilbert stood up, the back screen door to the house flew open, and the voice of Bobby's mom shouted, "Bobby! Why is Timmy crying? What did you two do to him?"

Bobby poked his head out of the tent. "We were playing a game, and he thought we were unfair with him."

"*Were* you?"

Gilbert poked his out, too. "No. We were playing fair. Timmy got mad because he got shot."

"Got shot? With what?" Her voice tensed.

"A Turmoil, Mom."

"A Tur*what?*"

"It's a made-up gun for the game, Mom. Make believe. You know Timmy gets upset easily."

"I know he does." Her voice softened. "Just let him win sometimes, okay?"

"We do! He thinks he has to win all the time!"

"Well, try and be easy on him, okay?"

Bobby let out a long sigh. "Sure, Mom."

"Hey, I got you boys some pizza if you want."

Gilbert and Bobby's eyes lit up. Even though they had already eaten leftover Manwich from lunch, two whole bags of barbeque potato chips, and a king-size chocolate bar apiece, their stomachs grumbled.

"Sure, Mom! Be right there."

"Okay. I'll leave it on the counter. I'm going up to take a bath."

"All right."

The screen door shut.

"Well, guess you'd better go pee outside after all, Gilbert."

"That's fine." Gilbert stood up and stepped out of the tent. The darkness hummed with crickets and other nightly sounds. A light in the bathroom upstairs flicked on. Below, the kitchen light blazed from behind a window with yellow drapes.

Gilbert began relieving himself and heard a twig snap. He whipped his eyes back and forth, trying to look into the darkness. But his vision brought him nothing.

Something rustled only a few steps from him. Hurriedly, he finished and zipped up. For a moment, Gilbert shuddered. His mind was creative, and with that said, it brought him an image of a wild animal crawling out of the woods after him.

It wasn't that Gilbert was a scaredy-cat, it was just the fact that there really wasn't much light in Bobby's backyard at night. And it was a bit eerie. The porch light only pushed away the darkness so far while the continuing sounds of what lurked in the dark of the woods stayed hidden from the naked eye.

Five minutes later Gilbert and his best friend entered the house and found three quarters of a pizza pie left. Timmy sat at the kitchen table devouring his second piece. He didn't speak a word to them for the rest of the night.

Later that night, while watching an old horror flick on TV in the basement, both boys fell asleep while huge cockroaches swarmed an entire town, attacking everyone. Each boy was unaware of the grinning face peering at them through the window, leaving not a mark of breath on the glass.

* * * *

Gilbert said his goodbyes to Bobby the next morning and walked home. He said he would return that afternoon after he'd done his chores. They both agreed to add bike riding through the trails on the agenda.

It suited them fine.

Walking home, Gilbert saw Mr. Houchin across the street mowing his lawn, and he waved at him. The old man returned the gesture and grinned. A few cars passed by and one vehicle thumped music from within, nearly vibrating the entire frame.

Today was Saturday. Both of Gilbert's parents were home.

Before Gilbert walked through the front door, he could hear the vacuum running. When he entered, his thin-framed mom was cleaning the living room carpet, her back facing him.

"Hi, Mom," he shouted. "I'm home."

His mom didn't even turn around, devoured by the task of moving the vacuum back and forth, sucking up dirt.

"Mom!" He raised his voice a little louder.

She still didn't turn around.

Gilbert walked up to her and tapped her on the shoulder. She jumped and her face whipped around, eyes wide. She shut off the vacuum.

"Gilbert! You scared me!"

"Sorry, Mom."

Her shocked expression eased up. "That's fine. Have fun?"

"Yep."

"What did you and Bobby do? Watch movies?"

"Yeah. A couple." Gilbert refrained from speaking about entering the house by the river. Mom would kill him. "And we played that game that Bobby made up."

"Dungeons and Dragons?"

"No, that was invented by two guys named Gary Gygax and Dave Ameson."

"Really? Huh." As with any mother—almost any—Gilbert's loved to hear her son talk about things while his eyes filled with excitement.

"We played the one Bobby and me made up together called Shank."

"I see."

"So, um," Gilbert looked over his mom's shoulder and down the hallway toward the bedrooms, "where's Dad?"

"Oh, now, you shouldn't have to ask me that."

"The garage?"

"Yep."

"Oh, okay. I'm going out to see him." Gilbert began stepping away until his mom stopped him.

"Hey, kiddo! No hug?"

Gilbert didn't mind giving his mother a hug—as long as he wasn't around other kids who, if they saw him doing it, would call him a mama's boy quicker than he could roll a twelve-sided die. Hidden inside his house, between the walls, he knew he was safe.

Unless some kid he didn't know had a super-duper telescope. However, he guessed that the word for such a person would be a Peeping Tom.

Gilbert embraced her, and she kissed him on the cheek. As he drew away and walked toward the back door, he heard the vacuum start up again. He had a few questions for his father about the house. Maybe he could sorta slip it by him, nonchalantly.

Gilbert saw the door to the garage wide open and noticed his dad's legs sticking out from under the front of the car that sat on two jacks. His dad was changing the oil in the car.

"Hey, Dad."

The legs twitched. A second later a tall man rolled out from under the vehicle on a long piece of hard plastic with wheels. His face had a smudge of grease on it. His hands held even more. "Hey, sport. Have fun last night?"

"Yeah. We had a lot of fun. Um, Dad?"

Gilbert's father got up, turned around, and dragged out a large plastic bowl filled with black oil that sloshed around the edges. Bending down to pick it up, he replied with a grunt: "*Yeah*, son?"

"Ummmm...I was wonderin'. What's up with that house down by the river?"

So much for being nonchalant.

Gilbert's dad paused in mid-step. Then he regained his movements, walked to the back of the garage and sat the bowl of oil down off to the side. "Why do you want to know, son?" he said, not turning around. "Both me and your mother have already told you to never go in there. Ever."

"Oh. I know. I was just wonderin' if there's a bad history there or not."

Gilbert's father glanced back at him. "Did someone *tell* you that?"

"No. I was only wonderin'."

"Gilbert." His dad grabbed a rag and started wiping off his hands while stepping over in front of him. "I'm not going to lie to you. There's a history in there, but I shouldn't tell you until you are older."

"Why not?"

"Well," he cleared his throat, swallowed, "it's a bit hard to explain. And I'm your father and I know best. Just promise me you won't go near that place."

The words were like a replay of his mother's. "Sure, Dad." So was the replay of Gilbert's fingers silently crossing behind his back.

"I only want what's best for you. Okay?"

"Sure. I won't go near the place," Gilbert replied with a small lie.

* * * *

The rest of the day went swell. Gilbert and Bobby teamed up and followed through with their plans and rode through the trails on their bikes. They even had time to stop at Harry's for ice cream—by far one of their favorite places to eat a double banana split with whipped cream and nuts and two cherries on top that came in an elongated bowl in the shape of a boat.

"So how are you boys on this fine sunny day?" Harry

spoke through teeth with gaps, standing at the order window inside his ice cream shop.

Both boys replied, "Fine."

"That's good." Behind Harry, four teenage girls wearing solid white uniforms, much like a nurse would wear—minus the white bandanas stretched and tied over the top of their heads—were busy making ice cream treats for other customers. Vehicles in the drive-thru coiled around the building and ended at the entrance/exit off the street.

Gilbert felt the cold air of the air-conditioning drift out of the window as he stepped forward to order. "We'd like our usual, Harry." He smiled.

"Mmmm. Let me see." The owner placed a finger on his chin. "If memory serves me right, you two want two small chocolate cones."

"No!" Gilbert's smile dropped, and a worried look pushed through. "We want a double banana split."

"You sure about that? I thought for sure you two would rather have two child-sized cones of ice cream."

"Yeah, we're sure," Bobby defended. When it came to eating ice cream, both boys meant business.

Harry smiled. "Aw! I knew you two wanted your double banana split. I just wanted to see what you'd say."

Gilbert and Bobby grinned.

"Don't mess with us like that, Harry!" Gilbert said. "We're serious about our ice cream. Right, Bobby?"

"Right," Bobby answered.

Harry guffawed. "I know you two are. One desirable, delicious, huge double banana split coming up."

Paying Harry, then retrieving the tasty morsel from the next window from one of the workers who barely even offered a thank you, Gilbert and Bobby sat at one of the concrete tables with a large umbrella hanging over their heads like a vulture.

"You know," Gilbert said as he scooped up his second cherry, "I really wonder what is up with that house."

"You mean if it's haunted or not?" Bobby spoke through a mouthful of whipped cream.

"Yeah. But I'd like to know its history. I still think I heard and saw something there last night."

"Probably nothing."

"Probably. But what if?"

"If what?"

"What if there's a ghost in there. Or many ghosts? It would be cool to go back and scout them out, you know? See if we can hear anything. We'd be heroes of the town!"

Bobby swallowed a spoonful of ice cream before he said, "It would be cool to check it out again. That was only our first time there. If there is a ghost, maybe we can communicate with it."

"Yeah! We could go back and try and be real quiet and see if we get a response."

"Without Timmy."

"*Without* Timmy."

"Good idea."

That evening after returning home, after eating dinner,

after watching TV, Gilbert turned in for the night. Around three a.m. a ghostly presence stood at the foot of his bed, its head lolled to the side, glaring at his sleeping body.

* * * *

The following week drifted by. Gilbert was stung by a wasp while out in his backyard, and it felt like a stake had been driven through his hand. He did not cry. Big boys did not do such a thing. However, wincing was allowed.

In the latter part of the week Bobby and Timmy got into a fight, broke an antique lamp that had been their grandma's, and were both grounded for two days and had to sit in the house with the bright sunshine teasing them through the windows. And, like mental telepathy, showing them that if they had not gotten in trouble, they would be basking in its warmth. So, Gilbert had to find other things to do during their incarceration.

When Friday arrived, though, the dark clouds parted and gave them a better end to a non-enjoyable week. This time, Bobby was spending the night with Gilbert, and they had hauled over the tent and set it up in his backyard. Gilbert's mom and dad had gone off to a movie, but not before informing them that there were Cokes in the fridge, potato chips in the cabinet, and chocolate bars in the freezer. Both boys loved to eat them frozen.

Despite how hard it was on the teeth to tear a piece off, it was well worth the wait as it melted inside their mouths.

As darkness crept into the evening, they found themselves standing outside of the old house that loomed over their heads like a giant constructed of wood, plaster, and glass.

"This place is creepier than the last time," Gilbert said as he opened the front door and the hinges screamed for oil. His flashlight's beam speared the darkness.

"No doubt!" Bobby replied and flipped his flashlight on, automatically bringing back a vulgar picture drawn of a naked woman with big—

"Boobs?" Gilbert asked.

"Yep. That's what they are. Well, I think that's what other kids have told me they're called."

"Wow."

Both of the boys stood there gazing at the picture, wondering what a real live woman would look like. Very naked.

"You know, my dad has some kind of magazines only for adults at his house."

Gilbert turned his head. "Really? What kind?"

"For adults only," he reminded his friend. "I think they're bad ones. Wonder if they have naked women in them or naked men? One day, I overheard my mom shouting at my dad on the phone to make damn sure to keep those pages of smut away from me. Man, they were arguing! She was pissed!"

"Smut," Gilbert repeated. He took notice that to speak the word you first had to use your teeth and tongue, hissing like a snake, then pressing your lips together to follow through with the action. It impressed him that he'd learned a new word.

"So, what does it mean?"

"Damned if I know."

Gilbert's memory flashed something. "I think Ralphie from school brought one of those kinds of magazines in. Got caught, too."

"No kiddin'?"

"Yep. I heard from John who heard it from Gary who heard it from Lisa that Ralphie was suspended for a week and got a beating-and-a-half from his parents when he got home. They said he couldn't sit down for a week!"

"So, he stood up all week when he ate and had to do number two?"

"Yep."

"Get outta here! No way! You can't stand up and poop."

Gilbert paused, let Bobby's words sink in. "Mmmph. You're right about that."

"You let people put too many weird thoughts in your head, Gilbert. Don't believe 'em!"

"Oh. Guess I shouldn't."

The two explorers shoved forward as a musty smell caressed their noses, almost bringing forth a sneeze. Meanwhile, they both noticed something.

"How come it's so cold in here, Bobby? It was awful hot outside today."

"Was it?"

"Oops. Forgot. You were stuck inside. Well, at least Timmy isn't with us."

"So true! He's at my dad's, staying the night."

"I've noticed you haven't been over there for a while."

"No. I haven't."

"What's up with that?"

The two started ascending the steps to the second floor, their footfalls echoing throughout the house.

"I, uh…just don't want to go over there. Dad has…uh, a girlfriend."

"Really? You've never told me that before."

"I'm not too happy about it. Neither is my mom."

"How long have they been divorced?"

"They're not yet. He's been gone a year, though."

Gilbert had heard that you should be divorced before you hook up with someone else. Or, at least he *thought* that was correct. "Man. That's weird."

"Yep."

Gilbert sniffed, rubbed his nose. "So, does this mean you don't like your dad's," he sneezed, "girlfriend?"

"Exacto-mundo. Not at all, dude."

"Huh." In Gilbert's mind, he could never comprehend the fact of his parents splitting up and his dad with someone else other than mom. It would be like mayonnaise and applesauce. Neither one goes with the other. Now, chocolate and caramel and nuts would be a much better fit!

To Gilbert, it would just be odd to have to keep going back and forth to each house. Would he have to choose which one to live with? He hoped not. He loved his mom and dad. The horrible thoughts of something like that really happening didn't sit very well in his gut.

"Girls. Who needs 'em? Huh?" Bobby asked.

Gilbert was pulled free of his thoughts. "Uh? Oh, not me!" He smiled.

"Me neither!"

The second floor seemed colder than the first, and it wasn't very hard for the two boys to realize it.

"Dang! I've got goose bumps." Bobby announced.

"Same here," Gilbert replied, rubbing his arms.

They stood in a long hallway full of open doors, the moonlight leaking in. The current of the river that ran beside the house could no longer be heard, nor could the other nightly sounds lurking about. Everything had grown gravely quiet.

"Set up camp here?" Gilbert asked.

"Sure. How much time do we have before we have to go back to your place?"

Gilbert stepped over to an open door where the moon shone through its window and he looked at his watch, squinting, trying to see the digital numbers from the moon's light. Then he remembered the tiny button on the side that lit up the display. He pressed it. "About an hour or so. Their movie started a few minutes ago."

"Think that'll be enough time?"

"Gonna have to be. I don't wanna be grounded, too."

"Point taken."

They sat across from each other and turned off their flashlights while the dark pressed against them. Only the light of the moon through the doors stayed. And the coldness seemed to worsen.

Bobby's voice drifted out of the dark. "After we stay here for a few minutes, we'll venture upstairs."

"Cool."

"That is, if we don't hear or see anything."

"Okay."

The sounds didn't come suddenly; rather, they slowly surfaced, bubbling over with the house spilling its guts. A door banged shut at the end of the hall. Another echoed the first at the other end. It made the boys jump each time.

"Wow," Gilbert whispered.

A breeze blew through the hall, kissing the boys' cheeks, and brought the smell of cookies, making both of the explorers' stomachs rumble. Giggling of children followed. The running of feet came next, slapping the floor in front of them, ending at the other end.

"This can't possibly be happening, can it?" Gilbert whispered.

"Yeah! I think it i—"

Each boy felt fingers all over his body, touching his face, feeling his arms, pulling his hair.

"Ow! Dang, that hurt!" Bobby snapped, rubbing his head.

"No kiddin'!" Gilbert agreed.

Next, heavy laughter came plummeting from down the hall, reverberating off the walls. At the opposite end it repeated itself. And then…silence.

"This is too weird, man!" Bobby whispered.

"No kiddin'! Wait'll we tell the kids at school!"

"Let's hope it's later than sooner."

"Don't you mean *sooner* than later?"

"Yeah. Same meaning though."

"Remember Mrs. Beel's class last year?"

"I'm trying to forget it! She made me stay after school and write on the chalkboard 'I will not fall asleep in class' fifty times! Ugh! Let's let not think about school. Let dead dogs lie, Gilbert. I would have rather not had that vision of the old bat!"

Gilbert chuckled. Wow, he thought, four cool words: *Let dead dog's lie*. "Sorry. You're right. We don't want this summer to end yet! We're havin' too much f—"

"Whoaaa!" Bobby's word cut Gilbert off. When Gilbert turned his head, he saw why.

Peeking out of a room ten feet from them was a black mass casting its shadowy form on the floor brightened from the moon. In the blink of an eye, the shape drew back inside.

"Look at that!" Bobby said.

Gilbert was speechless.

Something else peeked out of another door directly across from the first, then quickly sunk back inside.

"What the heck?" Gilbert said in a low voice.

"I wonder if those things want to communicate?" Bobby asked.

Gilbert gave no response. This was a lot for him to mentally swallow.

Bobby rose up, and Gilbert heard him and asked, "Where are you going?"

"I'm gonna see if I see anything in those rooms."

"Are you sure that it's *safe*?"

"Sure. What can they do to me? They're only ghosts."

Gilbert wondered if there was a danger in trying to communicate with the dead. Could they be bad ghosts? Could they be—he swallowed with a *gulp*—demons? And while that thought simmered, he saw Bobby's silhouette cross in front of one door, blanking out the shine of the moon. Then in front of another door until he arrived at the room where they had first seen something peeking out at them.

"See anything?" Gilbert asked.

At first Bobby was silent and didn't respond. Only stood there, his hands hanging down at his sides. Then he replied, "Nope."

Gilbert felt a bit of courage. "Stay right there." He got up.

"Hey! I see something! Wow!" Bobby's face lit up, and he stepped into the room.

Gilbert scrambled forward.

"Gilbert, you need to see this! Come here and check it ou—"

"What?" Gilbert now stood by the door and looked inside. "What do you s—" The room was empty. Only the broken window brought in a small breeze that invaded its space. "Bobby? Where *are* you?"

He saw a closet with its door shut.

Gilbert frowned. "Bobby! You trying to scare me or something?" He placed his hand on the doorknob and gave it a twist, opening it up to reveal a yawning darkness. "Ummmm...*o*-kay."

Something scurried over his foot. He jumped. Flicking on his flashlight, he saw a mouse run across the floor. "Bobby? Where are you at?"

Bobby's voice did not come. Nothing responded, either.

Gilbert walked out of the room and noticed that the place was eerily quiet, a small pause for the haunt. The air continued to stay cold, and the musty smell lingered.

Gilbert stood in the middle of the hall with a shiver rolling down his spine.

Behind him came running footsteps. Before he could turn around, a hand shoved Gilbert down to the floor. Before he could rise, another hand pushed his head down, followed with a giggle.

Fear shook Gilbert. He wanted to go home. He wanted to find Bobby and go home. He did not want to be here anymore. This was no longer any fun. So much for creeping around in a dark house, wondering if it was haunted or not—the question had already been answered. His and Bobby's hidden treasure, so to speak, had opened up its chest and poured out.

Finally rising, Gilbert bolted. He would have to call the police and tell his mom and dad when they returned home—*Boy, they were going to be mad! He wouldn't sit down for a whole week for defying them!*—about trying to find his best friend Bobby.

Gilbert tore down the hall, down the stairs, and headed for the front door. Heavy laughter sailed from above, cackling. When he pulled on the doorknob, it did not open.

More laughter came, morphing into small giggles.

Gilbert started for the back door in the kitchen. When he touched the knob an apparition of a long face appeared in the door's large window, smiling, showing off its hollow, sunken eyes.

Gilbert snuffed a scream. He backed away, dread draining into his frame. The face pushed through the glass, hanging in the air by itself, while everything below the chin slowly cascaded down into a slim figure of a man until it touched the kitchen floor.

The ghost cocked his head, asked, "You like to explore, lad?"

Gilbert's tongue felt swollen. His throat locked up. He couldn't answer.

"Do. You. Like. To. EXPLORE? I asked." The man's ghostly hand reached over, opened an empty drawer under the counter, pulled free a ghostly butcher knife.

Gilbert's feet stepped backward on autopilot, and it was like someone had dumped a bucket of ice over his head. Pulling away from him, drifting through his flesh, he saw the back of a woman's head with long hair. When she turned around, a thin smile formed under the pointy nose attached to her long face.

Gilbert's flashlight left his grip and hit the floor. Both of the ghostly figures were a bright, glowing white.

"What do we have here, my love?" the woman asked.

"An explorer, my dear. This boy thinks of himself as an explorer. Right, young man?" He licked his lips.

Gilbert felt frozen to the spot where he stood.

"Aw, he's scared, Phillip. Look at him! Cute little boy

afraid of a big man and a big woman?" she asked, her words followed with a cackle.

"Well, boy, are you exploring this house or not?"

"Uh…y-yeah…me and Bobby."

"Whom did you speak of, boy?"

"M-My friend. He's supposed to be with m—"

"There is another explorer here with you?" The ghostly face of the man beamed. "The more the merrier, I always say. Eh, Margret?"

"Yes, dear. More the merrier!" The lady let loose an eerie chuckle.

"So," Phillip stepped over, inches from Gilbert, looking down at him, "where is this *Bobby*? Upstairs? Into mischief?" Both hands were behind his back, and the thought of the knife he held soaked into Gilbert's mind. He didn't know if he was going to get stabbed or not. Would it cut him, being ghostly as it was? Hopefully not.

"Where is this Bobby you speak of?" Phillip asked again. "Huh? Into mischief?"

"No. Nothing like that. I can't find Bobby. He—*we*—were upstairs, and he walked into a room and disappeared and—"

"Disappeared?" Margret asked, standing beside her mate. "How so?"

"I don't know."

"Surely, boy," Phillip said, "people don't just vanish. Now do they?"

"They don't?"

"No. They do not. They couldn't unless they had some

help, you see." A grin spread under his nose. "Right, dear?"

"Yes, Phillip."

"People do not vanish into thin air," Phillip walked past Gilbert, "without our help. Boy?"

Gilbert turned to him.

"People vanished a long time ago with the help of me and my beloved Margret. We made history back then." He chuckled in a low, sinister tone. "Boy, it was something back then." He pulled the knife into view and ran his ghostly finger across its blade, letting his eyes drop. When he spoke again, his voice was nearly a whisper. "It was something to see. Yes, yes. So many frightened folk they were. So many deaths. But..." His eyes rose, as did his voice. "Now. Being the exploring type such as yourself, you would love to explore a floor that my Margret and I know deeply about."

"Yes," Margret agreed. "It'll be so much fun for you!"

"Come." Phillip motioned Gilbert forward.

Gilbert did not move.

"Come," Phillip demanded.

Gilbert still did not move.

Phillip let loose a long sigh and said, "Dear? Would you help this child along?"

"Glad to." She placed two hands on Gilbert's back and pushed him. He stumbled forward.

"Okay. Follow the leader," Phillip said and laughed.

Gilbert, sandwiched in the middle of the two ghosts, followed the man while his lady stayed in tow up the staircase all the way to the second floor. There, the air was like ice.

"I'm going to let you walk down that hall," Phillip pointed, "and look inside each doorway, understand? Each one will have an unburied treasure!"

Gilbert wanted to go home. He wanted to find his best friend. He did not want to be under the roof of this house longer than he had been. Maybe he could try to escape and get away from these two.

"Go on. Seek out your fate, lad."

Gilbert looked at him.

"I mean...seek out your treasure."

The woman cackled.

The hallway was very similar to the first floor—including the open doorways spilling out the light of the moon. And Gilbert's feet did not want to budge. They wanted to rocket out of this haunted house. Immediately! Visions of a cartoon character's feet spinning like the wheel of a car came to his mind.

"Boy. I told you to move. Now!"

Gilbert found his feet nearly moving on autopilot again— or was it that fear had finally taken hold of them, and they were merely doing what they were told or else? The "else" being something he did not want to find out. What would these two ghosts do to him if he didn't move? Try and cut him with the ghost knife?

The hall was very long and ended in darkness without the help of the glow of the moon. It looked like a pitch black pit. Beyond that was anyone's guess—well, actually, Gilbert's. That was one place he would rather not tread. As he moved he could have sworn he heard a moan close by. It chilled him.

Passing in front of the first doorway, he did not want to look inside, and instead kept his face forward. He was afraid of what he might see.

"Not interested in any sights to see, boy?" Phillip asked.

"N-No," Gilbert stammered.

"Come now. Being an explorer like yourself, don't you want to see what is in that room?"

"Oh, but you must see!" Margret said with excitement in her voice. "Shouldn't he, Phillip?"

"Yes, my dear."

The moan returned from inside of the room.

Gilbert swallowed down a dry throat. Tears filled his eyes, but they did not drain. Big boys did not cry.

"Oh, it's not going to hurt you, boy. Look. Now!" Phillip barked.

Gilbert shut his eyes, heard the moaning blossom like a flower, and twisted his head. When he opened them, he nearly lost his balance from the shock. Inside was a ghostly young lady gagged, tied to a bed, spread eagled. She thrashed back and forth, trying to free herself.

Then two familiar figures entered the picture. One stood over the woman with his long knife, while his beloved stood on the other side. Before the door slammed shut, the beloved's face glared at Gilbert and grinned as the man whisked the knife through the air in an arced descent, heading for the piece of meat tied to the bed.

Gilbert covered his eyes and backed against the wall.

There was a scream.

"How about that, boy?" the man asked.

Dropping his hands, Gilbert saw that the murdering duo still stood at the start of the hall, grinning from ear to ear.

"All right. Now, on to the next," Phillip said.

Gilbert did not budge. His mind wondered if he could run past them and escape. To his right he was reminded of the darkness at the end of the hall. He started thinking strongly about it, too.

"Move those young legs. Now!"

Phillip's command shoved Gilbert over to the next open doorway. He closed his eyes. He did not want to open them.

"What's wrong? Don't want to see inside that one, either?"

"No!" Gilbert was surprised at his own voice echoing off the walls. Fear had pushed the word through his throat.

"Oh, but you must look at that room," Margret insisted. "It is something to absorb into your vision, child." She giggled.

Gilbert disobeyed.

"Open your eyes, boy. Or I'll cut them out," Phillip's voice boomed.

Tears filled Gilbert's eye sockets with one lone tear slipping out from under his eyelid, streaming down his chin.

"I said look into that room!" Phillip's voice was so loud that Gilbert could have sworn he felt the vibration of it.

He opened his eyes.

And saw an empty room. No figure tied down on a bed.

No moaning to be heard. The room was as vacant as a hollow coffin.

Laughter came from the two. "Did you see his expression, Margret?" Phillip asked. "The boy was in complete fear!"

"Yes," Margret replied and chuckled, "he sure was!"

Gilbert felt an anger rising in his chest. He was being used as a pawn in some sick game. He rubbed his eyes and face and glared at the two.

"Well? What are you waiting for? On to the next." Phillip shooed Gilbert with his hand.

The darkness at the end was not very far away. Not. At. All.

Gilbert's feet stepped to the next door as instructed. He heard moaning again. He also heard a voice, a muffled whine: "Help me, please..."

"Look inside, boy!"

What spilled into Gilbert's eyes was more horror than he wanted to take in. The walls were splattered with blood. Whatever was in the room on the floor had been gutted like an animal and skinned. A mutilated figure of a male or female—he had no idea which—squirmed in its own pond of blood. Fragments of bone lay all around, stained crimson.

Gilbert took off. He passed by three more rooms—*was that machinery I heard?* he wondered—and into the darkness at full speed.

"Stop! Now!" Phillip's voice boomed. "Get that boy, Margret! Get the damned soul back h—"

His words vanished as Gilbert was submerged in the

darkness. He kept his pace, running for his life, until the moon's glow came back, spilling through a doorway in the hallway as he arrived at the end of the hall. There was nowhere else to go.

As he twisted around on the ball of his right foot, his eyes were drowned with the darkness he had just run through, slithering back down the hall very, very slowly and revealing where he had just tread. Minus the two apparitions who filled his mind with terror.

So, cautiously, he walked toward the stairway.

* * * *

Gilbert refrained from peeking in each room. He did not want to see any more horror. As he continued forward, the hall seemed to stretch and never end. Or was that only his imagination? Had the hall originally *been* that long?

He blinked, rubbed his face with his hand.

Finally, just as he was about to make it to the stairs, he heard a sound behind him. Fear of the duo standing in the middle of the hallway bled through Gilbert. He had hoped they were gone for good.

Another sound, the shuffling of feet.

Taking a deep breath and letting it out, Gilbert slowly turned. It wasn't the couple who stood there, but a boy nearly his own age clothed in bib overalls and a faded t-shirt underneath. A small rip had separated the collar and fabric right below the boy's chin.

"Hey," the blond-haired boy said with a smile.

"Um. Hello?" Gilbert replied.

"I know where Gilbert's friend is."

The words didn't have to sink inside of Gilbert's brain very long before a warm feeling sparked under his chest and he responded with: "You do? Where's he at?"

"The other side."

A cold finger touched the middle of Gilbert's spine. For Gilbert, the other side could mean death. Well, that was what his grandma would always tell him about where Grandpa was.

Gone.

To the other side.

…in Heaven.

The thought of his best friend dead, he could not fathom. There was no way Bobby could be! "The other side?" Gilbert asked.

"Yep. With a capital O and a capital S." His "s" hissed. "I can show Gilbert. I can! I can!" A layer of excitement surfaced in the boy's voice.

"Where is this…Other Side? Can you actually get to it?"

The boy blinked and did not say a word for almost a whole minute, as if he were trying to narrow down a short-ened version of a long story. He finally opened his mouth, grinned, and said, "Steven will gladly show Gilbert."

"Who? And how do you know my name?"

His smile dropped, his head bent to the side. "Why, eve-ryone knows of you, Gilbert."

"Um. *O*-kay." The situation was getting weirder by the minute. And the memory of his parents' words telling him never to step foot in the house came back to haunt him.

The boy motioned for him to follow with a wave of his hand. "Steven will show Gilbert where to find his friend Bobby."

"All right." But the feeling of something bad coiled up like a snake ready to strike inside Gilbert's gut. He didn't like it one bit. "So, your name is Steven?"

Ignoring the question, the blond-haired boy rocketed down the hallway.

"Wait up!" Gilbert shouted as he took off too, and followed close behind.

The boy slipped into one of the rooms, and the door slammed shut.

Gilbert stopped. He looked at the door. From behind it the boy's voice called for him: "Gilbert! Come on! Steven knows where Bobby is! He is in big trouble! Hurry up, slow-poke!" Followed with a giggle.

Gilbert opened the door and stepped into the room—or rather, into a large field full of tall grass that grew way above his head.

* * * *

Okay. Where the heck is he? Gilbert wondered. The boy had disappeared.

Up in the sky the sun was out, laying the rest of its shine for the day as it slowly made its descent for the evening.

Gilbert had no idea which way to go because he could see only a green wall of tall grass all around him. And where was his leader?

"Over here, Gilbert," the boy's voice boomed somewhere off to the right. He started weaving his way through the grass, trying to find exactly where the voice was coming from. It had rained, saturating both the grass and ground, drawing out the strong smell of the grass as if it had recently been cut.

"I'm close, Gilbert. Hurry! We haven't much time!" the boy's voice boomed again.

Gilbert stumbled after his foot sunk into a shallow indention on the ground, tweaking it a bit, but he pressed on. When he closed in on the voice and made his way over to it, he didn't find the boy. Instead, while his face contracted into a frown, he bent down and picked up a small tape recorder the color of silver. Through the small speaker it coughed out a few more words in the boy's voice. There was a click, and the tape ended.

Gilbert was speechless. And very, *very* confused.

The boy's voice hollered out: "Gotcha!" Then he guffawed and followed with: "Sorry. Had to do that! Come on over in this direction, you'll see me!"

If memory served Gilbert right, the boy had just told him there wasn't much time to find Bobby. Why would he be playing games?

Gilbert sprinted through the tall grass, finally finding the voice once again coughing out the last words through the small speaker of a chrome-colored tape recorder. Poor Gilbert had not a clue.

"Over here!"

"Where are you *at*? Tell me where you are, Steven!" Gilbert cried.

"Over here!" the boy's voice echoed from Gilbert's left.

"Over here!" the boy's voice echoed from Gilbert's right.

"Steven! Quit it! Please tell me where my friend is," Gilbert snapped.

"Over here!" the boy's voice thundered, coming in all directions at once. Gilbert had no idea where to look.

"Please tell me where you are, Ste—"

"I am not only Steven. I am someone else, also." There was no laughter after the statement. Solid words that touched Gilbert's skin like ice-cold rain, making the hairs on his arms stand erect. He shuddered.

"Then, *who* are you?"

"You will soon...find...out...*boy*." The words were drowned out by a low vibration that first seeped into the bottoms of the tennis shoes Gilbert wore, crawling up his legs until he soon felt it reach the top of his head. The feeling was very odd, as if Gilbert had placed his sock-covered feet on the top of his mom's vacuum cleaner and felt its vibration— though this was much worse, as if it could surely rattle the bones beneath his flesh.

Slowly, it grew louder. Something was heading straight for him, tearing up grass and shooting it high in the air. The ground began to rumble, and Gilbert wasted no time just standing there, waiting for whatever came toward him.

He sprinted through the large blades of grass, every so often hitting wet puddles, with water slapping his bare knees and seeping into each shoe.

The vibration changed into a persistent hum that made the hairs on his neck stand up. It was a domineering force that made his flesh crawl.

And added to the mix was a continuous swishing sound growing rapidly.

Gilbert ran as fast as his legs would carry him. But where was he running to? Where could he run to in this green maze? His vision was still blinded by a wall of green grass, and he was not tall enough to peek over it and look for an escape route.

The ground rumbled, almost making Gilbert lose his balance.

The swishing continued to grow, invading the air, tucking into the canals of Gilbert's ears. He was tiring out. More puddles. More water slapping. Sometimes even sprinkling him in the face with every footfall. The rank smell of the grass seemed to cover his face like a mask, leaving a bad taste on his tongue and coating the inside of his throat.

Behind him, whatever pursued this eleven-year-old boy was closing in for the kill like he was a hunted animal.

Gilbert denied his thoughts of glancing over his shoulder and losing distance. Nope. He would very well lose that minute he could not snatch back.

Pistons inside of a machine worked fiercely, knocking loudly, spewing exhaust into the air, seeking out Gilbert's ears. Belts spun rapidly. The ground increased its rumble. The vibration had not stopped; instead, it had gotten worse.

Out of breath, tired, his body ravaged with a soreness creeping up his legs, Gilbert knew he could not go on much longer. There had to be somewhere out here to duck into and hide.

Relief suddenly reached out and sucker-punched him.

The ground rose up, slanted down in a slight decline, and a huge oak tree appeared surrounded by the tall grass. Slats of wood had been hammered onto the trunk for access upward like a makeshift ladder.

Gilbert saw it and immediately began to climb. His finger tips barely gripped the thin boards, but he pressed down, feeling one of two of his fingernails scrape the wood, and scrambled upward until he reached a tree house that had seen better days. Half of it was gone, including the roof, as if a huge pair of jagged teeth had bitten into it. It sat inside the palm of odd-looking branches that grew vertically, as if each were fingers trying to reach the sky, with green leaves growing off the stems.

Once Gilbert had made it, he shifted around and peered down at the one who chased him. Or, rather, the "it" that chased him. His pupils looked very large inside the whites of his eyes as they grew wide.

Down below through the leaves was not only a combine harvester used to harvest crops, but a robotic one at that. The front of it held a long, skeletal frame of steel cylinders, with sleek blades that spun rapidly. The unit itself was bulky, box-like in shape, and sat on an all-terrain chassis. Behind two dark-tinted windows was a vacant seat in the cab where a driver would normally sit.

"INTRUDER," a voice boomed out of the machine, "YOU HAVE BROKEN LAW 128 CODE 7 OF THE BOOK OF BLOTH. GIVE YOURSELF UP. NOW."

It wasn't it a question, either.

Gilbert was stunned. He wondered what would happen if he did not give up. He wondered what would happen if he, say, just stayed up in the tree. Thoughts of that thing trying to cut the tree down snaked through him.

"INTRUDER. GIVE YOURSELF UP. YOU HAVE BROKEN THE LAW AND MUST BE TRIED IN A COURT OF LAW."

Tried? In a court of law? Heck, he was still a child—I mean a big boy.

"IF YOU DO NOT COME DOWN, I AM IN-STRUCTED TO BRING YOU DOWN MYSELF. HOW-EVER POSSIBLE."

"Get away from me!" Gilbert's voice was weak, shaky, but it held meaning. He hoped.

"THAT IS NOT THE RIGHT ANSWER."

"So? Leave me alone!"

"UNDER BARON LAW YOU MUST BE BROUGHT BACK AND TRIED IN A COURT OF LAW. NOW."

"I haven't done anything wrong! Where am I?"

"YOU HAVE TRESPASSED ON PRIVATE PROPERTY. YOU HAVE BROKEN ONE OF THE BARON'S LAWS. COME DOWN AT ONCE. I WILL NOT ASK AGAIN."

The words cut through the air. Gilbert knew he was beaten. He did not want to die, if that was this rust bucket's option of the law. "How do I know you won't kill me?"

"I AM ORDERED BY THE BARON HIMSELF NOT TO. IF I FAIL I WILL FACE DISMANTLING."

Gilbert did not know if he should believe it or not. But at this point, what choice did he have? He took a deep breath, let it out. "Okay. I-I'm coming down."

Grease and the thick smell of diesel fuel filled Gilbert's nostrils. He screwed his face up at it. Slowly, he made his descent by climbing back down, carefully gripping the slats of wood. Before his feet were ten feet from the ground, he felt a steel clamp gently squeeze him around the waist and lift him up.

"Hey!" he shouted, trying to struggle free. "I said I was coming down!"

"THIS ASSURES YOUR CAPTURE. DO NOT FIGHT IT. REST, HUMAN BOY."

Gilbert did what he was told. A cover on top of the cab automatically slid open, and Gilbert soon rested his bottom in a leather seat before it closed back. Two seatbelts shot out from one side and clicked themselves on the other side, holding him in snug. One lay across his chest, the other across his legs.

"Is this necessary?"

"YES. YOUR SAFETY IS MY CONCERN. IF I ARRIVE BACK WITH YOU DEAD I WILL BE DISMANTLED AND SCRAPPED."

A lump formed in Gilbert's throat, and he pushed it down and asked, "D-Did you say dead?"

"YES."

The word did not sit well. Before Gilbert could wonder why on earth this machine would tell him something like that, steel plates slid over the front, hiding the cylinder-shaped skeletal frame and its blades. There was a loud pop, and two short wings with airplane engines slid out of both sides. The wings became vertical, the engines glowed orange, and the combine lifted off the ground. Gilbert's body flattened against the seat as he and the machine shot upward. One hundred feet in the air, the wings twisted horizontal, and the combine shot forward.

The world whisked by through the windshield. Far off in the distance lay mountains. The sun beat down, but with a climate-controlled environment inside the cab set on about sixty-five, Gilbert barely broke a sweat. Rather, he felt as if he was drying up—including his shorts that were wet from running through the puddles of water.

The machine leaned to one side, switching its direction.

Gilbert still felt flat against the seat, and he wondered what was going to become of him now. Where was this contraption taking him? Who was this Baron guy? And what was this book of Bloth that this hunk of bolts spoke about?

Unfortunately, Gilbert knew those questions would be answered soon. They were about to roll out the red carpet for him. Whoever *they* were.

The machine slowed up and dropped suddenly. Gilbert felt his stomach drop, much like it had when he rode that rollercoaster last summer, at the moment it shot down the track after climbing up the huge hill. He had barely made the height required to ride it, too, checked by standing next to a wooden cutout of the amusement park's mascot, their fictitious character, Ernie the elephant. On the way to the park that day, Gilbert had laughed when he saw billboards off the road with pictures of Ernie riding a Ferris wheel, its large body stuffed into the seat. Another picture showed Ernie riding a rollercoaster, fitting snugly into a seat, sharing it with a little girl. Other people, all smiling and happy, sat in the cars behind them with their arms and hands in the air. Gilbert thought that had been false advertisement because whenever you rode anything in the amusement park, the rules stated to keep your hands inside the car and to hold onto the bar that fit across your lap. And there were the signs along the roadside showing everyone that it was okay to break the rules.

Not actually a good thing.

Now Gilbert felt himself lean forward and shoot downward in a vertical line. The ground below filled the view through the windshield as Gilbert clamped his eyes shut. The fear of crashing slammed into his mind.

There was a jerk forward, then backward. When Gilbert opened his eyes he was landing on a massive, flat rectangular piece of steel. Huge cylinder-shaped towers sat in the distance with green lights blinking off and on at their tips.

Gilbert felt another jerk forward.

"OOPS. SORRY 'BOUT THAT. I'M NOT SO GOOD AT LANDING. HAVEN'T PERFECTED IT YET."

"Um. That's okay, I guess." Gilbert wasn't really sure what he should say. He was being taken somewhere to be judged and then sentenced to…what? Death?

The flying combine had landed on a large red X. There

was a loud pop, and the ground began to lower into the steel landing pad. Shiny metallic walls filled the cabin's windshield as they descended downward. Gilbert had a horrid thought of being buried alive in a metal box.

Five minutes later the ride stopped. A door on the left side of Gilbert slid open. All this time, he had never noticed any hinges or anything of that nature. It was very odd to him.

And it was about to become much worse.

Two guards armed with rifles stood outside the door. Their uniforms were colored silver and black and they wore helmets, hiding their faces.

"Please step out of the vehicle," one said with a flat tone.

The seatbelts hadn't loosened. "Um. I can't. I'm still seat-belted in," Gilbert said.

"OOPS. SORRY 'BOUT THAT. FORGOT. TOO WRAPPED UP IN HAVING FUN RIDING DOWN ON THE ELEVATED PLATFORM." The seatbelts released. "I HOPE YOU ENJOYED YOUR RIDE. PLEASE TELL THE BARON WHEN YOU SEE HIM THAT I WAS CAREFUL. AND IF YOU WISH TO FILL OUT A COMMENT CARD, I WILL PROVIDE ONE."

"Um. Okay. Maybe I will."

Wasting no time, the combine produced a thick slip of paper that slid out of a thin hole on the dashboard. Gilbert grabbed it and read it. Five questions were written. One asked if the ride was comfortable. One asked if they driver was polite. One asked if you ever felt you were in any danger along the way. One asked if the climate inside the cab was pleasant. And the final one asked if you would refer anyone else to ride in this machine. At the end of each sentence you only needed to circle "Y" for yes or "N" for no.

Gilbert was speechless. This hunk of bolts wanted him to comment on whether the ride was an overall pleasant experience while he had no idea what kind of judgment awaited him? Was this thing for *real*?

"Please step out of the vehicle," the guard repeated in his flat tone, and Gilbert could have sworn he heard one of the rifles click.

"I'm comin'! I'm comin'!" Gilbert grumbled as he stepped out of the combine.

"GOOD DAY," the voice of the machine told Gilbert as he was led through double doors and into a long hallway. He could see no doors on either side of him, only plain white walls. However, there were different pictures of the same man posed in different settings. One picture showed the guy leaning against a guillotine with a bloody blade. One picture showed him holding a huge, bloody two-sided axe over his shoulder. And one picture, rather disturbing, showed him strangling a young lady who had long but died. Her ash-gray face was turned toward the camera, her eyes were slits, and her mouth was agape with her swollen tongue hanging out. And as Gilbert was escorted farther, he had to tear his eyes away from even more disturbing sights.

In each of the pictures the man had been grinning from ear to ear, a sinister expression rippling across his face. From a close observation, one could figure that he wore thin flesh around his bones. Dark military clothing wrapped his frame, which could give one the thought of Death himself. The only thing missing was a long scythe in his hand.

At the end of the passageway, Gilbert was led through two more double doors and up a flight of steps until they stepped through a single door and into a large room with dim lighting.

"Sit right there, boy," one of the guards said, pointing to a seat in the middle of the room.

Gilbert obeyed and sat.

The guard turned and joined the other while they stepped back out of the room. As soon as the door was shut, a small metallic sphere about the size of a basketball appeared, hovering in front of Gilbert. A line of green lights spun around the middle of its frame.

"*Brrrrgggggggtttt*," it sputtered a garble of something through a small speaker, followed by a squeaky voice crackling, "UNDER BARON LAW YOU ARE TO STAY SEATED UNTIL JUDGED. *Brgggttttt*. DO NOT ATTEMPT TO LEAVE. DOING SO COULD RESULT IN BEING SHOT ON THE SPOT."

Nice, scary words, Gilbert thought. He stayed put and didn't chance it. Anyways, where would he go? He was like a mouse caught in a mousetrap.

The sphere hovered in the air a little longer, as if waiting for him to defy the demand and try to run, coughed a sentence out that Gilbert had no idea what the heck meant, and flew off to the side.

Gilbert gazed up and couldn't see the ceiling, if there was even one to begin with. The place was a little chilly. Shadows lurked from the dim lights. Gilbert wanted to go home so bad he could taste it. He still wondered what had happened to his best friend. Bobby had to be around here somewhere—he hoped.

Minutes later a tall figure materialized out of the dark and sat down behind something directly five feet from Gilbert. The lights rose, pushing back the shadows, and Gilbert saw that he now sat in a courtroom. A very small jury appeared off to his left side, made up of six robots with faces like gas masks and silver bodies for their frames. Each had two large black circles for eyes, one large circle similar to a fan under them.

Gilbert did not like the eerie look of them. He had never actually seen a robot in person besides the combine.

A little old lady with reading glasses across her nose, which kept sliding down while she repeatedly pushed them back up, sat to his right at a desk in front of an old typewriter, acting as the court reporter.

The judge behind the bench held a stern face. He was an older gentleman who reminded Gilbert of a mean old man who lived around the block from his house. The guy never left his porch light on for trick-or-treaters and always chased any kids off who were ten feet from his front door.

The judge's eyes fell on Gilbert. "I am the judge, prosecutor, defense, uh…" He glanced down at something on his desk. "Gilbert. Mmmph. Funny name. Where did you get such a name as that, if I may ask?"

"My mom and dad gave it to me."

"Were they on drugs?"

Gilbert had to think about it before he spoke. Was he talking about prescribed medication, like pills? "Um. No. I don't know."

The judge leaned forward, and Gilbert suddenly felt as if he were a teeny-tiny spot on the floor. "Either your reply is 'yes,' 'no,' or it's 'I don't know.'"

Gilbert was silent.

"Well? Which is it, boy?"

"I guess it's 'I don't know.'"

"Mmmph. Well. That figures." He leaned back.

"What is *your* name?" Gilbert asked.

The judge stared at Gilbert for a very long time before he spoke. "You may address me as Judge. To others, I am Horace."

Gilbert chuckled. Whoever heard of a *Horace*?

Horace the judge gave Gilbert a very mean expression that made Gilbert clam up. "I would advise you, boy, to not call me that or laugh. Understand?"

"Y-Yes, sir."

"It is 'yes, Your Honor.'"

"Um. Yes. Your Honor."

"Good. Now, let us proceed. The court calls Jacob Kef-fels to the bench," the judge's voice boomed.

From behind Gilbert walked an older guy dressed in bib overalls who took a seat at the bench. The guy took off his straw hat.

The judge turned to him. "Do you solemnly swear to tell the truth, the whole truth, according to the Baron Law?"

"Yes, Your Honor." His voice held a country accent.

"And if you do not choose to do so, you are well aware that you will be taken outside in the courtyard and put to death by an electric chair?"

"Yes."

"Good. Please proceed with your complai— Wait!" Horace's eyes fell on the old lady in front of the typewriter. "Maggie."

The old woman's head was hanging forward, as if she were asleep.

"Maggie." The judge's voice was louder.

No response.

"MAGGIE!"

The old woman twitched, and her head popped up and her eyes flew open. "Y-Yes, Your Honor?"

The judge stared at her for almost a whole minute before responding. "Time to go to work."

"Y-Yes, Your Honor." She got herself straightened up, and her fingertips fell on the keys.

"I apologize, Mr. Keffels, Maggie must have a wire loose. May need to recharge herself after this session. Now. Please proceed with your complaint."

Recharge? Gilbert thought. Like batteries? What's Horace talking about?

The old man cleared his throat. Coughed. "This mornin' I was sittin' at m' kitchen table eatin' breakfast when I saw somethin' movin' out in m' field."

Maggie's typewriter made a *tap-tap-tap-tap* sound that filled the courtroom.

"What exactly did you see, Mr. Keffels?" the judge asked with a hint of his expression changing. Though one really couldn't tell if it was concern or merely an attempt to be polite.

"Well. I saw a boy trespassin' out there. I'd ah sent out m' old dog Bert, but he's too old to go-a-chasin' people off." He chuckled and dry coughed. "Some days I don't think he wants to hold a charge."

Charge? Gilbert thought. What's that supposed to mean? Battery charge, maybe?

"So, anyways, I leave the boy be. 'Sides, my legs ain't what they used to be. Can't go runnin' out there in that tall grass."

Tap-tap-tap-tap.

"Can you point out the boy in this courtroom, Mr. Keffels?"

"Sure." His eyes found Gilbert. "There he is! Right smack there in that seat lookin' at me with a scowl!" The old guy pointed a shaky finger at Gilbert.

Scowl? Gilbert wondered what that word meant.

"What did you do then, Mr. Keffels?"

"Well." He sniffed and turned back to the judge. "I got on the line an' called the authorities, and they came out an' I explained to them what was goin' on."

"Very wise decision, Mr. Keffels." The judge glanced over at Gilbert with an unreadable, blank expression.

Gilbert felt a lump in his throat.

"They told me that they would be glad to take care of the matter. So, they sent that big robut out there to get 'im."

Tap-tap-tap-tap.

"Right." The judge pushed a few buttons on his desk, and it appeared he was looking at a computer screen. "They sent the Gleemer 120 after the boy."

"Yep. That's right. Wish I had somethin' like that to cut m' grass. It was a humdinger!" He addressed the last sentence at the jury.

They sat there as silent as a graveyard.

"Thank you, Mr. Keffels," the judge said, "you may step down."

"My pleasure." A wide grin spread under his nose.

Tap-tap-tap-tap—pause.

The old guy stepped down, and when he walked by Gilbert he said with a hiss, "I hope they throw the Baron's Book of Laws at you!"

Gilbert was taken aback. And very scared.

"Jury? Have you made a decision?"

One robot stood up holding a flat, rectangular device and said, "Yes, sir," in a monotone.

"Please send me the decision in hyperlink mode."

The man punched in a few buttons.

"Thank you," Horace said, peering down on his desk. Then he looked up and said, "All rise."

Gilbert and the small group of robots in the jury stood up.

Maggie did not. Her head hung forward, and her fingers rested on the keys.

"MAGGIE!"

Maggie was startled so badly she jerked and her fingers flew, tapping on the keys. Gilbert could have sworn he saw one of her eyes spin in its socket.

"MAGGIE!"

She abruptly stopped and looked over at the judge. Then she quickly stood up, adjusting her dress.

Horace sighed, shook his head. "Maggie, go see Plymuth and get a recharge after this session."

Maggie nodded.

"Now, in the case of trespassing on private property and mowing Mr. Keffel's grass——"

Cutting his grass? Gilbert thought. I didn't cut his grass. That bucket of bolts did!

"——I find you guilty and sentence you behind bars for no longer than nineteen years."

Nineteen years! Gilbert cried inside of his skull.

"And during that time you will work as instructed up until your Conversion."

Gilbert gasped. Conversion?

"Then, afterward, your body will be used where needed."

"Conversion? What are you talking about? Why would you send me to prison, Judge? I'm only a kid!"

The judge flashed a mean glare at Gilbert.

"Your Honor?" Gilbert swallowed.

"You trespassed on private property. You must be detained and thrown in prison for your crime. You should already know what 'Conversion' means. You were taught that in your younger years."

"*Younger* years? I'm eleven years old! I was never taught what Conversion meant!" Gilbert pleaded.

"Then," Horace grinned, and it was not a pleasant one, "you will find out when you reach the age of thirty. As an eleven-year-old boy you will fit right in. You should have thought about your actions before you broke the Baron's Law."

The lights lowered and a shadow fell over the judge's face, clouding it. Soon, darkness covered the entire room, and Gilbert could not see anything in front of his face. Two straps fell across his frame, locking him in much like when he rode in the Gleemer 120, and held him snug in the seat.

Under him, he felt the floor shift. A line of yellow light circled him in the shape of a rectangle. Slowly, the ground beneath him lowered. First, it was slow. Then it dropped like an anvil.

Gilbert let loose a scream.

Seconds later he landed in a room with walls made of stainless steel and a door that slid apart, revealing two armed guards dressed in the same attire as before. The straps that bound him were released and the guards hauled him down a long corridor, through another sliding door, and into an infirmary, finally depositing him beside a hospital bed.

A tall doctor in a bleached white lab coat walked up, with a nurse in tow who pushed a cart holding five syringes.

Gilbert did not like needles.

"Hello, er, is it…Gilbert?" The doctor had pulled out a small device with a screen and read it.

"Yes."

"Funny name. Welcome to the Baron's prison." He slid the device in the front pocket of his lab coat. "We hope your stay here will be pleasant."

Pleasant? Gilbert wondered.

"Before you are taken to your cell, we need to inject you with four different vials of medicine. If we don't, you could very well die of disease."

"Wh-What kind of disease?" Gilbert's eyes widened at one of the injections the nurse picked up, sliding off a slim red cap and revealing a long needle. She lightly pushed the plunger, and a thin spray of medicine shot into the air. With two fingers, she flicked the side of it, bursting the tiny bubbles.

"Well, there's a flesh-eating disease for one. Another is a disease that eats your brain. None of you children are any good to us if either of that happens. We want you well to be able to do the work that is needed."

"Work?" The word didn't seem to fit into Gilbert's vocabulary. He was a kid. He liked to have fun and go outside and ride his bike and go to bed late and not get up until he wanted to. That is, except during the school year.

"Yes. We will need you to work during the day and get plenty of rest at night. Now. Pull those britches down and bend over."

Gilbert didn't move.

"It will only be worse if you fight, Gilbert," the doctor said with one eyebrow raised. "You don't want these two guards to make you, correct?"

Gilbert watched as the guards tightly gripped their rifles. "I...guess not." He turned around and pulled down his pants so that his bare butt showed.

"Okay. Don't move. It'll all be over quickly."

And it was not quickly enough for Gilbert. Each injection felt much worse than the penicillin shot he had had to receive in the emergency room when he was very sick. Each injection burned like a lit match when the medicine went into his skin. Each injection felt like a wooden stake was being driven into his skin. If they had sawed off one of his hands, Gilbert felt that it would have been less painful. Probably.

Afterwards, both guards had to sling their rifles over their shoulders and drag Gilbert to his cell.

And there, he met a new friend.

* * * *

"I'm Rodney."

Rodney's head hung down off the top bunk with his big blue eyes wide in his sockets and a large grin spread under his nose. His blond hair hung off his scalp like the top of a palm tree. He held out his huge hand to Gilbert.

Gilbert had no idea how long he had lain there. The guards had escorted him into the cell and the world had disappeared for awhile as he went to sleep. Hearing movement in the cell, he woke up.

"I'm Rodney." The large kid was still stretching out his huge hand.

Gilbert offered his hand and it was like a clamp that gripped it, swallowing whole. Rodney shook it fiercely, shaking Gilbert's entire frame.

Rodney let go, and when he spoke again, his words were slow. "Rodney has no friends here. Be my friend?"

"Um. Sure. Guess so," Gilbert muttered, rubbing his left cheek on his butt. It was one big bruise from all the shots, so he eased himself up on his right side.

Rodney twisted around, climbed down, and plopped on the floor in front of Gilbert. "I've been in here a very long time. Why are you here? Um...what's your name?"

"Gilbert."

"Mmmph. Funny name."

Gilbert frowned.

"Where did you get it?" Rodney asked.

"My parents."

"Oh. My mom and dad didn't name me. When I was born, they sent me away to the orphanage."

"Orphanage?"

"Yep."

"Why?"

"'Cause I was different."

"Like how?" Gilbert rubbed his eyes and glanced around at the steel walls of the window-less cell and saw one toilet made of steel, one small steel table attached to the wall, and what looked like a small refrigerator.

"Well. If I tell you, you may not want to be my friend."

Gilbert looked at him and saw a sad expression clouding Rodney's face. "I don't see why I wouldn't want to. I don't know anyone else here."

"They call me a...retard." Rodney closed his eyes and winced as if someone was going to strike him, like an abused pet.

Gilbert knew that word well. Back at his school, there was a class for kids who were slower at learning than the others. And he hated when some of the mean kids, like Byron Freetly, the bully every kid knew, would tease them. Whenever Gilbert saw this, he'd ball both fists up with an anger flaring inside his gut and defend them—and usually end up in the principal's office for starting a fight. Freetly would somehow get off scot-free and end up being the kid who was only standing there minding his own business when Gilbert had walked up to him and pushed him down.

"Well, Rodney, I'll be your friend." Gilbert smiled and watched as one of Rodney's eyes opened.

"Sure?"

"Yeah."

"Positive?"

"Yeah."

"With whipped cream and a big cherry on top?"

Gilbert chuckled. "Yes. I need someone to talk to. I shouldn't even *be* here."

Rodney tilted his head to the side and frowned. "Shouldn't *be* here?"

"No. I'm not from this place."

"Where are you from, then?"

"Another world. Me and my friend Bobby were walking through a haunted house, and he disappeared. I went looking for him and encountered two mean ghosts."

"Ghosts?" Rodney's eyes were wide.

"Yep. Some really bad ones, too. They terrorized me, but I got away from them. Then I ran smack into a ghost of a boy who tricked me into following him through a door into his world. Your world—wherever it is."

"You ran into him?"

"Yeah, and he tricked me."

"If he's a ghost, you wouldn't run into him, right?" Rodney frowned. "You'd go through him, I've always heard."

"I didn't actually run into him. It's a figure of speech, Rodney. I confronted or came upon this boy."

"Oh. I see! So, you aren't like an alien or something?"

"No. I wouldn't quite call me an alien. Don't know what to call me in this world."

"You are human, though. Like me."

"Yeah."

"Well," Rodney licked his lips, "how did those two ghosts terrorize you, Gilbert?" He opened the door to the small refrigerator.

"They showed me people—I think—that they killed a long time ago."

"Whoa!" Rodney's eyes were wide, and he held a chocolate cupcake in his hand. "That's scary."

"Yep. Anyways," Gilbert continued, noticing how good the cupcake looked, "I was caught trespassing in a field by a robot of some kind, judged, and placed in here."

"You went before the judge, too?" Rodney said through a mouthful of cupcake. "Wow!"

"They sentenced me to nineteen years. Nineteen years, Rodney! I can't do that! I wasn't even doing anything wrong!"

"In this world you can break a law very easily."

"Really?"

"Yep. I broke the Baron's Law, and now I'm here."

Gilbert noticed other prisoners talking, far away from the cell. "What did you do?" he asked. "What are you in for? And who is this Baron dude?"

Rodney's face held an expression that made Gilbert draw back a bit. He smiled, showing the whites of his teeth, and replied, "Cannibalism."

It was as if the world flipped upside down. Gilbert felt fear ooze into his pores. The word brought back the meaning of a human who eats another human. An animal that eats another animal of the same species. Gilbert had seen too many zombie movies, too. He had been taught in school about the cannibals overseas in other countries. He had been taught that those people were—

"—nice to Gilbert."

"What? Wh-what did you say?" Gilbert had zoned out.

"I said Rodney wants to be nice to Gilbert." Rodney's face was back to normal. "He is Rodney's new friend."

"But. You are a *cannibal?*"

"Yep. Always have been."

"Um. Okay. That's just weird."

Rodney's eyes widened, and a shock lay across his face. "Oh! I see why you are actin' like that!" He held up his hands. "I never eat my friends!"

"Y-You don't?"

"Nope. I eat bad people. You're safe with 'ol Rodney."

"I, uh, hope so."

"PRISONERS. IT IS TIME TO EAT," a voice boomed through loudspeakers out in the hallway, and the cell door slid open.

"Oooh! Time to eat!" Rodney shouted and rose up, headed toward the door.

Gilbert didn't move. "Eat *what?*"

Rodney glanced over his shoulder. "Food. Hamburgers, hotdogs, chicken. What else is there, silly? C'mon. Let's go, Gilbert!" The big kid stepped over and grabbed Gilbert's arm and yanked him to his feet. "I'm very hungry!"

"Bet you are," Gilbert said under his breath as he stepped out into the hall. Many other kids were out there, all dressed in prison attire. And now for the first time, Gilbert noticed that he wore the same thing, too.

When had he changed? Or did they change his clothes for him?

"Hey, Rodney! Who is this Baron guy?" Gilbert asked, but Rodney was nearly sprinting down the hall, not hearing a word he said.

* * * *

After catching up to Rodney, Gilbert slowed down and walked with his new friend to the cafeteria along with many other prisoners. Each prisoner was young, like Gilbert and Rodney. Guards stood on each side, facing forward at attention, their rifles in their hand, their fingers resting on the triggers.

A strong aroma of food hit Gilbert's nose as two double doors opened. Ushered inside, following the pack, they stepped into a large room that already held a lot of prisoners, all kids, who were in line receiving their plates of food. Some were even taking their seats at long tables.

"Which do you want, kid? Chicken or beef?"

Gilbert and Rodney had gotten in line and now faced a rather large woman wearing a uniform, an apron and a hairnet stretched over her head to hold down her thick gray and black hair. She wore way too much makeup and her eye shadow was running under her eyes, as if they were bleeding black.

"I guess beef," Gilbert told her.

She didn't crack a smile or say a word while opening up the lid of a metal container and using tongs to pull free a flat beef patty, placing it on a hamburger bun that sat on a plate. She slid it to the next person.

"Fries or vegetables, kid?" another large woman asked, dressed similarly to the other. Minus the heavy shade of makeup.

"Fries," Gilbert replied.

The woman never cracked a smile, either, and slid the plate to the next person who, this time, was a thin, older man. "Drink?"

"Um. Do you have Coke?"

"Nope."

"Grape soda?"

"Nope."

"Red soda?"

"Nope."

"What about lemonade?"

"Nope."

"Ice tea?"

"Nope."

"Then, what do you have?"

"Water and prune juice."

Prune juice? Yuck! He screwed his face up in disgust. It gave him memories of his own grandma sipping on a glass of it, telling him it helped her constipation. When he had asked what that word meant, he wished he hadn't. Kind of made him sick to his stomach.

Gilbert picked up the plate with his hamburger and fries and decided on the large glass of water, picking it up also. He had to lag behind and wait for Rodney because he was still trying to make up his mind if he wanted fries or vegetables.

"Make up your mind, kid. We don't have all day, you know," the cafeteria worker grumbled.

"I know. I don't know which one to pick," Rodney replied.

She rolled her eyes.

"Hey. Retard!" a kid's voice hollered behind them, standing in line. "Make up your stupid mind!"

A wave of anger smacked Gilbert. His gaze found a tall

boy, about twelve or thirteen with short black hair and freckles. Two kids behind him looked to be his friends, egging him on, whispering and smiling.

"Hey, retard! Can you guess what one times one times one is?" Before Rodney could answer, the kid said, "Ooops! Guess not! Not smart enough to figure it out, huh?" The kid guffawed. So did his accomplices behind him.

Rodney glanced back at him with a sad expression plastered across his face. He made up his mind, got the fries, didn't pay any attention when they handed him prune juice, and brushed past Gilbert and plopped down into a chair at an empty table.

Gilbert sat down across from him. "Why don't you do anything about that? Why didn't you say anything back to them?" he asked.

Rodney's eyes flicked up at Gilbert, and they were watery. "I dunno. Rodney can't take that kind of punishment very well. Never could."

"You need to yell at those kids! They are mean!"

"I know," Rodney said in a low voice, nearly a whisper.

"Stand up for yourself!"

"Rodney has before. But I always goof up. I end up...um...eating them."

Gilbert paused for a long moment. "Do what?"

"Yep. That's why I'm here. Been in three different prisons to try and rehabilitate me."

"No kiddin'?"

"Nope." He sniffed.

Gilbert felt bad for Rodney. Since he was an actual cannibal, it sort of scared Gilbert; but if he really ate guys who liked to tease him or torment him, well, maybe that was his only defense mechanism. Sickening, dreadful, and very nasty, but maybe he just needed to learn how to pop a guy in the nose so he wouldn't mess with him anymore. Gilbert wasn't sure what the answer was.

Rodney had finished his burger and was working on his fries when a tall shadow fell over him and Gilbert. Both boys looked up to see the tall boy with the black hair and freckles standing there, along with his cronies standing behind him.

"I guess retards *can* make up their own mind, huh?" He laughed. So did his friends.

Gilbert stood up.

"Oooh! Rodney got a friend?" The tall boy's eyes looked at Rodney, then at Gilbert. "I'd watch yourself around him. He eats people, you know? Crunches up their bones and drinks their blood."

"So?" Gilbert surprisingly found himself saying. "You had better watch it, or he'll eat you too."

"I'd like to see him try it!" the boy snapped.

"Why don't you leave him alone?" Gilbert's patience was beginning to wear thin. "Go eat your food."

A couple of other kids who had sat down to eat had twisted around and were looking at the two.

"Maybe I don't want to. Why do you want to defend this freak, huh?"

"Because," he glanced at Rodney, who hung his head low, "he's my friend, and I'm standing up for him."

Rodney perked up a little, a smile growing under his nose.

"Your *friend*? That thing sittin' right there?" The boy pointed to Rodney. "You must be as nuts as he is. He's just a retard. A nothing!"

Gilbert balled up his fists that hung at his sides. "Take that back! Don't call him that!"

"What?" The boy stepped forward, nose to nose with Gilbert. "What are you gonna do about it if I don't take it back, huh? You're probably a sideshow freak like him! Look at you," his eyes crawled over him from head to toe, "you have something sickening that you like to do? Do you eat your own poop or something?"

Gilbert's anger bubbled in his chest.

"Do you and Rodney," he whispered, "touch each other down the— *Uggh*!" The boy's words were cut off, and he found himself lying flat on the floor. His two friends were in awe.

Gilbert stood over him, his right fist raised for another blow. His first two knuckles scraped the kid's front teeth.

Everyone in the cafeteria who had been talking stopped. All eyes were on the two.

"Kid, you are gonna pay for that!" the tall kid said through a bloody mouth and jumped up and swung at Gilbert, but missed. Though his other fist, in a left hook, shot out and connected with the side of Gilbert's jaw.

Gilbert went sprawling into a table.

Kids were getting up; some were walking over to the fight scene.

The two boys who were the bully's accomplices stepped forward and grabbed hold of Gilbert.

"Hold him, Munch. Twitch, bend his arm back!" the tall kid shouted. "Kid, you are gonna feel pain like you haven't before!"

Struggling, Gilbert replied, "I already have. I have to look at you, don't I?"

"Hold him still!" the bully shouted as he moved in.

A large crowd of kids began circling around the scene, shouting, "Kick the crap out of that boy!" Gilbert had no idea if they were talking about him, or the bully.

The tall boy managed to land a punch in Gilbert's gut with Munch and Twitch holding him upright. He gasped for air. Another blow landed in the same spot, and the world spun. Right before another blow came, it was caught and the kid was hauled backward.

Rodney stood there. His face no longer sad, it had twisted into a sinister expression. It gave Gilbert a chill along his spine. It was as if Rodney's unhappiness suddenly drowned in a lake of madness.

"Hold 'im!" Munch spat. "I'm gonna get this freak! He ain't gonna do this to Vinnie!" He had only stepped forward two feet before he was lifted up by his neck by that huge clamp of a hand Rodney had and tossed aside like a ragdoll. Munch's body bounced off a table and smacked the floor.

Twitch let go of Gilbert, and he slid to the floor. Then he took a stab and attacked the big kid. Rodney sucker-punched him, and the kid's nose flattened; he went sprawling backward, lost his balance and landed on his butt. Twitch cried out, holding his nose.

"Gilbert!" Rodney shouted.

Gilbert was trying to swallow the fact of what Rodney had just done, that quick, in a matter of seconds.

"Gilbert?" He looked up at Rodney. "We need to go. The guards will be here soon."

"Where? Where can we go?"

"Leave it to Rodney. He knows the way." Rodney smiled, his sinister face now wiped clean.

Gilbert and Rodney took off, pushing through a crowd of kids, down a long hallway bleached white.

From behind them, Vinnie, Twitch, and Munch shouted: "I'm gonna find you two, and when I do, I'm gonna get YOU. BOTH OF YOU!"

* * * *

"Um, where are we going, Rodney?"

The two ran down a long hallway without a hint of any doors to be seen.

In between breaths, Rodney replied, "We're-going...down this...way."

"I can see that! Where is *this* way?"

"There's-a-door...down...here...to-go...outside."

"Then where?"

"Into-the...woods."

67

"Oh."

Suddenly the hallway was filled with swirling red lights bouncing off the walls, and a siren screaming.

"Is that an alarm?"

"Yep. For us. When…tries…to-escape…it…goes…off."

"What happens if they catch us?"

Rodney didn't answer.

The two turned down another passageway, took a right, and through a large window Gilbert saw people lying in beds. A light over each headboard shined down on them. Their arms and hands lay across their chests as if they had been laid to rest. Gilbert didn't know if they were dead or not.

"What was that back there?" Gilbert asked after they had passed.

"Tell you later," Rodney replied.

They took a left and came to a door.

"What happens if they catch us, Rodney?" Gilbert asked again.

The big kid glanced over his shoulder at Gilbert and said, "They'll shoot us or place us in front of the axe-wielding squad or in an electric chair or do something bad to us."

Gilbert remembered when the judge had told the farmer about being placed in an electric chair if he did not tell the truth in court. If that didn't give Gilbert a chill, he proceeded to think of the axe-wielding squad Rodney had mentioned. "Um. Wielding means, like, *swinging*. Right, Rodney?"

"Yep. Sometimes instead of a firing squad, they use axes to chop people up. It's messy."

A picture of someone standing there blindfolded with their hands tied behind their back and being hit with more than one axe, sunk into his brain. The aftermath was gruesome. "J-Just like that? They'll kill us?"

"Yep. We gotta go. C'mon!" Rodney swung the door open and motioned Gilbert with one of his big hands to follow him as they ran down a long flight of stairs.

* * * *

Wide pipes ran on both sides of Rodney and Gilbert. Small lights stuck up into the crevices of the wall, flickering, not giving off much light. Somewhere, water dripped.

"Where *are* we?" Gilbert asked.

"Underneath the prison and the city, where the Baron lives."

The two had stopped running and were walking briskly.

"City? I never saw any city when they brought me here."

"It's built underground. Aren't they all?"

"No. Not where I'm from."

"Oh. That's weird."

"Not for me it isn't."

The passageway looked very long and held more darkness than light.

"So, who were those people in the rooms back there, Rodney?"

Rodney didn't turn around when he said, "They are robots."

"Robots? They looked human to me."

"Every year there is a lottery, and six adults between the ages of twenty-five and thirty are chosen to be turned into robots."

Gilbert's parents were thirty-five and thirty-nine. If they lived here, they'd probably already have become—

"Robots," Rodney explained, "are what the Baron uses for his guards and other tasks. He used to have human servants, but they would only get hurt or die off or disobey and try to run. But not with robots. They obey the master."

"Huh. That's, uh, weird," Gilbert replied, thinking about the guards who'd ushered him into the prison. He wondered if the nurse and doctor had been mechanical, too.

They came to a T, and Rodney stopped and scratched his head. "Can't remember which way to go."

"You don't know?" Gilbert asked.

"Can't remember."

"Can't remember? Have you done this before?"

"Yep. But got caught."

"Wait. You've tried to escape before, and they didn't use an axe on you?"

"No."

"Why not? I thought you said they would kill us by chopping us up or placing us in an electric chair?"

"No. I said they would kill us by chopping us up or shooting us or do something bad to us."

Gilbert blinked twice, confused a bit, and said, "Do what?"

"Do what, *what?*"

Gilbert shook his head. "Rodney, I'm trying to figure out how come you are still alive."

"Oh. Because they didn't kill me."

"That part is obvious. Why didn't they?"

"Because they did something bad to me. A near death torture."

"Which is…"

"They stuck me in a chair and gave me a few jolts of electricity. Enough to shake me up and stun the heck outta me."

"Oh. So they used the electric chair."

"Yep, but didn't turn the knob all the way up. If they had I'd be a roasted pig."

"Didn't it hurt?"

"Yep. But they told me next time I'll be killed if I try and escape."

"Well, then, we need to keep moving. I don't want to get electrified."

Rodney smiled. "Not to worry, Gilbert. Since you are with me, that makes you an accessory. They won't electrify you at all."

"That's sorta reassuring."

"They'll just chop you up into little pieces with an axe."

Gilbert had no words to add to that.

"Okay," Rodney said. "Which way, mmmm, which way to go? Oh. Wait! I know! C'mon, Gilbert, this way!"

Rodney sprinted off and Gilbert stood there, still stunned from the dreadful words of being chopped up.

"C'mon, Gilbert!" Rodney snapped and Gilbert blinked, waking up out of his daze, and took off and followed his friend through a long patch of darkness.

"Watch your step," Rodney said. "There's concrete stairs leading down here somewhere."

"Down? Why would they lead *down*? We are in the basement."

"Basements always have another level below them."

"Not usually."

"Sure they do. You didn't know that?"

"Not where I'm from."

"Sounds like you're from a very weird place, Gilbert."

"Look who's talking," Gilbert said under his breath.

"What?"

"Nothing. Hey, where's the steps you're talking abo—" Gilbert's feet slipped out from under him; he landed on his butt and did a roll down concrete steps until he bumped into Rodney, who stood there looking down at him with the bangs of his hair hanging in front of his eyes.

"You okay, Gilbert?"

"Yeah. I think so," he groaned. "Feels like I've been run over by truck."

Rodney reached down his huge claw and helped Gilbert stand up.

"If a truck ran you over you'd be dead," Rodney said.

"I know. It's a figure of speech," Gilbert explained.

"How can you figure speech?"

"Um…" Gilbert was at a loss for words. "I don't know. It's just something I've heard other people say."

"So, does everyone say funny things like that where you are from?"

"Sometimes."

"Oh." Rodney scratched his chin.

The room they were in had lights along the walls. The place looked like a junk area with metal racks against the wall and old prison clothing sitting in piles. Other objects, not recognizable to Gilbert—metal pieces or tools of some sort—were strewn all over the floor.

"Which way now?"

Rodney looked to his left, to his right, and replied, pointing with his thick finger, "Let's go that way."

The two started off again, and the lights slowly became a distant memory as if the dark had pushed them away.

"Wish there were more lights," Gilbert said. "I hate not seeing where I'm goin'. How about you, Rod—"

"Shh!" the big guy hushed him. "Hear that?"

Surprisingly, Gilbert had not. Until the sound came back with a scratching along the walls. "What's that? The hairs on the back of my neck are standing up!"

"I think it's the rats."

Gilbert paused and allowed that to sink in before he replied, "Did you just say r-rats?"

"Yep. Big ones."

"You've seen them?"

"Last time I was down here. That's why I couldn't escape. They took chase after me, and I freaked out and turned back around."

"Rodney, how mean are these rats? Can we fight them off?"

More scratching drifted out of the darkness and gave the two a chill, as if invisible fingers lightly caressed both boys' backside. They both twitched.

"We can run from them, Gilbert. I don't want to try and fight them off."

"Isn't there something in here that we can use to defend ourselves? I saw a long pole back there when there was light. Maybe we can turn around and go ba—"

"No! If we go back they may get us."

"They may get us now!"

"No, I don't think they will. C'mon, let's keep moving."

"Rodney!" Gilbert felt a wave of frustration. "I hope you are right! I hope we can get outta here soon!"

"We will. Follow me!"

Further into the depths of the level below the basement, the scratching became louder, more persistent, involving the addition of scurrying that sounded close to them.

"Um. Rodney?"

"Yeah."

"Is there a light at the end of this tunnel?"

There was a long pause before Rodney spoke again. "We aren't in a tunnel, Gilbert."

"I know we aren't. I'm asking if the way out is close."

"Oh. Another odd saying. Sorry... Um, it *should* be close."

"I hope so." Gilbert was losing faith in his new friend. He wondered if he should just turn back around and take the punishment of that dreaded electric chair Rodney had spoken about.

Wait, hadn't Rodney said he would be chopped up? Anyways, he didn't want to be down here in the dark anymore with the rats he could only hear and not see. He wanted to find Bobby and get the heck back home. He wanted to get back home and see his parents and never ever go back into that house!

Gilbert bumped into Rodney. "Hey! Why'd you stop?"

"Think I found the door." There was sound of a *tink-tink-tink* and the door slid open, revealing sunlight. Rodney glanced back at Gilbert and began to say something; then his bottom lip trembled.

"What's wrong?" Gilbert asked.

"D-D-Don't look behind you. L-Let's go. Right now!" Rodney shot out of the doorway like a bullet and ran off into a large wooded area.

Gilbert followed, but had to sneak a glance over his shoulder. And wished he hadn't. His eyes widened and his mouth froze in an O. In the doorway a mass of huge rats filled the floor only inches away from where the back of his feet had been. They had been very close, very near, hunting the two. Each rat had black beady eyes and a long snout and perky ears.

And, they were robots.

Gilbert stepped up his pace and allowed the woods to swallow him whole.

* * * *

If the tree he'd climbed earlier had looked odd to Gilbert when the robotic combine had captured him, the limbs grown in a vertical angle off the trunk, now he saw some that made sense. Sort of. They looked more like what he was used to seeing in his world, but were massive. Gilbert felt like a bug compared to them. They grew out of the ground and climbed the sky.

"Rodney," Gilbert craned his neck back to look upward, "these are some very huge trees."

"I know," Rodney replied, walking through dead leaves that scattered the woodland floor.

"Look at those bushes! They're bigger than me!"

"I know."

The two had been able to slow down, now that they were far away from the door where the rats had been. Rodney had told Gilbert that he thought they were safe right now, explaining that the rats would not pursue, as they kept out of the sunlight. From above came the sound of birds flapping their wings.

"This place looks like a giant lives here."

"I know."

"So, where are we going?"

"As far as we can. Don't want to get chopped up."

"Me neither, but I need to return to my world. I need to find my friend. I want to see my parents again." He paused, sighed. "Have any suggestions?"

"No. I'm sorry, Gilbert. I really don't. Maybe we'll find someone who can help you."

Gilbert sighed again. "Hope so. I need to figure out how to get back."

"There's a town at the end of the woods."

"Really? Good. Maybe there will be someone I can talk to."

"Could be."

"Wait." Gilbert stopped walking. "How do you know of a town?"

Rodney took three more steps before he, too, stopped. "'Cause I've been there before."

"Right. Guess that was before you were stuck in prison."

"No. I found out about it the first year I was put in jail."

"The first year? How long have you been there?"

"Ohhh, 'bout ten years."

"And you've escaped twice?"

"Yes. But I like to sneak out sometimes and go for a stroll."

Gilbert frowned. "You sneak out often?"

"Actually, a lot."

"But that's escaping!"

"No it isn't."

"Yes it is!" Gilbert snapped. "If you are supposed to stay locked up, you aren't supposed to be able to escape!"

"Not if you go back after your stroll."

Gilbert tilted his head to the side, scratched it. "I'm confused, Rodney. Back in my world, if a convicted dude is ever locked up—"

"What's a dude?"

"It means a man. A boy. A guy. You. Me."

"Oh. *Dude*," Rodney said, forming the new word with his tongue. "Neat word!"

"Anyway, if a dude is locked up, he stays locked up. He never gets to leave for anything."

"Mmmph. That ain't no fun!"

"Rodney, the guy is a danger to society. He's not supposed to get out."

"I guess I am too, huh?"

"I would think so, being a cannibal."

"Oh."

They began walking again.

"What about the rats that chased you, Rodney? Back there I figured you just turned back around and went back to your cell."

"I did. That was the second time I saw them."

"Second time?"

"Yeah. I had only encountered them once. Until a few minutes ago."

"I see. So," Gilbert pressed, "how many people have you actually eaten?"

Rodney thought for quite awhile before he spoke. "Maybe...four?"

"You've eaten four whole people?" Gilbert gasped.

"Or...was it five?" Rodney stopped, placed his fingertip on his lips.

"Five?"

"Mmmmm...six, seven, eleven... You know," Rodney chuckled, "I've lost count."

"Y-You've eaten that many people?"

"Uh. Yep."

"I hope you don't eat me!"

"Why would I? You are my friend. I've told you before, I

only eat bad people." Rodney smiled, and the thought of human flesh passing through his lips, of Rodney crunching down with those teeth, made Gilbert ill to his stomach.

"We need to keep it that way, Rodney."

"We will." After his words he turned and walked away, leaving Gilbert standing there a moment, until he took off and caught up with him.

Oddly, the farther they traveled into the woods, the more the sunlight that shot rays through the trees began to diminish. Night was coming fast. And to Gilbert, the place became gloomy.

"The town should be close, Gilbert."

"Good. So, how far have you gone?"

"Huh?"

"How far have you been from the prison?"

"Just to the town and back."

"Oh. Okay."

Before darkness shrouded the area, Gilbert and Rodney left the woods and entered the town. To Gilbert, it looked right out of an old western. Shops lined each side of the dusty street.

"So, this town isn't built underground?" Gilbert asked.

Rodney glanced over his shoulder. "No. Why would you think that?"

"Because of the prison and city behind us underground. What else?"

"Not towns. They are built above ground."

"I see that now."

A wooden sign stuck out of the ground, slightly tipped to the side, that read: *BASTEEL. POPULATION ABOUT 1000 MORE OR LESS.*

"More or less? What does that mean?" Gilbert asked.

"Depends on who has died yet."

"People die often here?"

"Yep. Sometimes every twenty minutes. But they come back, you know."

"Come back?"

"Yeah, they become recharged, good as new!"

"Um. Recharged? I'm not following you very well, can you explain that?"

Rodney didn't reply to Gilbert's question. Instead he turned his head in the direction of music drifting out of one of the doors. "C'mon, Gilbert." He motioned with his hand and walked up to it. "I think we'll be safe in here."

Gilbert nodded and followed him over the threshold.

Inside, light threw shadows on the walls. People sat along the bar and at the only three tables in the place. A few people turned to look at the visitors, then went back to playing cards. In the corner a guy played a keyboard instead of a piano.

"Rodney!" the tall, bald bartender shouted as each of the boys sat down on barstools. "How the heck are ya?"

"Great!" Rodney beamed. "Here's a good friend of mine. Gilbert. He's a prisoner like me!"

Gilbert gave a wave with his hand and said, "Hi."

"Good to meet ya! I'm Walt. Any friend of Rodney is a friend of mine." His brown eyes fell on Gilbert, and his head twitched to the side and back in a quick jerk. "Did you say your name was Gilbert?"

"Yeah," Gilbert replied.

"Huh. Funny name."

Gilbert frowned. "So I've been told."

"So," the bartender folded his arms over his chest, leaned forward on the bar, and twitched his head to the side and back, "what are you in for? Kill someone? Slice and dice some pretty woman? Steal some batteries? Rob a grave and take the loot?"

"Um. No! Nothing like that!" Gilbert was taken aback. "They said I was trespassing on someone's property."

"Really?" Walt's eyes were huge. "That's a mighty big offense for a young boy your age. Could have got the death penalty out of it."

"Death penalty!" The thought of being hacked into little pieces came drifting into Gilbert's brain.

"Yep. The Baron don't take kindly to people trespassing on someone else's property."

"Is the Baron really *that* mean? He wouldn't kill a kid...would he?"

"Let's just say"—Walt's head twitched again. He stood back, grabbed a shot glass and started wiping it with a towel—"that he thinks all children are mischievous little brats. That's why he's so hard on them. Like you and Rodney."

"So, what about all the adults?" Gilbert couldn't figure out if all this uncontrollable twitching bothered him or not. It was just...odd.

"What about them?" Walt defended.

"Well, don't they get into trouble, too?"

Walt looked at Rodney with a twitch of his head. "What's up with your friend? Sounds like he isn't from around here."

"He isn't," Rodney said. "He's from somewhere else."

Walt's eyes rolled back to Gilbert. "Where you from, boy?" he said with a twitch.

"Another place. Not like here."

"What's your place like? What's it called?"

"Well..." Gilbert had to clear his throat before he spoke again. "I live in a town called Deputy Point."

"Deputy Point? Never heard of it." Twitch. "Hey. Wait a sec. Looks like you need a drink. Rodney? Need one too?"

"Sure," Rodney replied.

Walt took two cold mugs and after two more twitches of his head, poured them both up with prune juice. He handed them over to the boys. Gilbert peered down into the glass and made a face.

"Don't drink prune juice, Gilbert?" Walt asked.

Rodney sucked his down.

"Uh. Nope. Kinda disgusting. Don't you have water or a Coke?"

"Coke? What's that?" Twitch.

"It's a soft drink."

"Soft drink?"

"Yeah. Not a hard drink, like beer, but a soft drink like...uh...Kool-Aid."

Walt frowned, confusion rippling over his face. "Kool-Aid?

Never heard of it. We don't serve beer no more. Baron's rules. Only water and prune juice and those cans of oil."

"Oil? Um. Do you have water, then?"

"Sure. Hang on." Walt's head twitched as he grabbed another cold mug, turned around to a sink and ran a faucet that poured brown water. He handed it to Gilbert.

Debris of metal or dirt, Gilbert did not know which, floated in it.

"Um. Maybe I'll just drink my prune juice."

"Okay. Suit yourself. That's the best water money can buy."

"Really?"

"Yep. No charge to you two though. So," Walt said with a double twitch, "where is this Deputy Point?"

"It's in Indiana." Gilbert wondered why Walt had not answered his question about grown-ups getting into trouble. And why did he continue to twitch his head?

"Where's Indiana?"

Gilbert took a sip of prune juice and had to push it down his throat before he tried another approach, asking, "Can you tell me where *I* am?"

Walt looked at Rodney, then back to Gilbert. "You are in Sector Three, Baron Country."

"Oh."

"The prison is Sector Two. Then there's Sector Four, Baron County."

"Huh."

"I'm surprised Rodney didn't explain it to you." Twitch.

Gilbert opened his mouth to reply and was cut off by Rodney. "He never asked, Walt. Anyway, I didn't know that the prison was Sector Two."

"I see," Walt continued. "There's even a Sector Five and Six. Again, it's all Baron Country."

"No more than that? It ends there?" Gilbert asked, trying to swallow another sip of prune juice.

"Well, as far as what we've been told." Twitch.

"Who has told you?"

"Why, the Baron of course. It's in his book of laws called the *Book of Bloth*."

"I've heard of that." Gilbert had remembered when the robotic combine mentioned to him, right before being imprisoned. "Do you have a copy of it?"

"Sure do." Walt reached under the bar and brought back a flat computer screen. He tapped the screen with his finger and it lit up, showing the wallpaper of a setting sun. Walt tapped a small icon twice and opened a file inside of a folder. The entire screen became white, with only the words "THE BOOK OF BLOTH" written in black capital letters in the middle of the page.

"You can read a little if you want," Walt said and used his finger to scroll to the next few pages.

"Can I try that?"

"Sure." Twitch. "Help yourself."

Gilbert touched the screen and, at first, the screen flipped ten pages forward.

Walt chuckled. "It is a bit sensitive. Watch." He took his

finger and, barely touching it, moved the pages back to the beginning. "Now you try, Gilbert. Don't press down too hard on the screen. Be easy with it."

It took a few tries to get it down, but Gilbert cracked the code, so to speak. He flipped through the acknowledgements on the front page and the part that read, "All rights reserved. No part of this book may be reproduced or transmitted in any form or by any means without permission of the Baron. The penalties to do so would result in disciplinary actions up to and including death."

Gilbert shuddered. He pressed on, flipping to the next page, where it began with the first sentence explaining the word Bloth: "Baron Laws of The Hearth."

He looked up at Walt. "What's 'Hearth' mean?"

Walt cocked his head, twitched, smiled. "Hearth is where we are. This planet is called Hearth."

Hearth? Gilbert thought. Was that the same as Earth, only dropping the letter "H" off the word? He continued further and read a long text, explaining what civilization was before this book and why it was written and implemented. Scanning a few words and phrases like "war," "the end to democracy," "terrorism in the last part of the twenty-second century" and "death to humans on Hearth," Gilbert had the feeling there had been a huge war and most of the population had perished. Farther down the page, he read something about the Conversion of humans to robots, per the Baron. It said nothing about the lottery Rodney spoke of, only the Conversion—whatever that word meant.

"Walt? What does this word here mean?"

Walt looked where Gilbert's finger pointed. "Conversion?"

"Yeah. What's that supposed to mean?"

"Well, I guess not being from around these parts of the Sector like yourself—or any other part of the Sector, from what it sounds like—means that every human is converted over into a robot."

Gilbert cocked his head to the side. "Robot?"

"Yeah." Twitch. "Nearly the majority of the planet's population in the Sectors is converted over to machine. Cogs, belts, fuses, batteries, the whole works."

"Nearly?" Gilbert glanced at Rodney and found he had finished a second prune juice and wore a purple mustache. "Did you know about this, Rodney?"

"Sure," Rodney replied. "Everyone knows. Thought you did too."

"No! I didn't know that!" Gilbert eyed him suspiciously. "Are you a robot, too?"

Rodney sat there a minute before he said: "Not me. Not yet."

"Not yet?"

"Not until I am of age."

"How old do you have to be?"

"Mmmph. Depends."

"Depends?"

"Yep." Rodney smiled.

"Depends on what, Rodney?"

"Depends on if I live long enough in the prison and don't die off before I reach the age of thirty. Or I'm chosen in that lottery they have every year."

Gilbert blinked. Swallowed. "Live long enough in prison?"

"Yeah. Prison isn't for everybody, you know. It's a rough place."

"Then how the heck have you survived this long?"

"Well, no one messes with me 'cause they know I like to eat human flesh."

"But those other kids, Vinnie, Twitch, and Munch hassled you!"

"Well," Rodney shrugged, "they always do. I hate when they do that, too. It sucks."

"They always do it?"

"Yeah. They are the Minis."

"The what?" Gilbert was sliding into confusion.

"They're Mini-robots. They are programmed to push people's buttons, hassle kids, cause trouble. If they weren't there to do it, no one would."

"You mean we just fought off robots?"

"Yep. Fun, huh?"

Gilbert's jaw still hurt a bit. He wondered if he wore a bruise. "No, it's not fun! This is madness!" Gilbert shook his head and covered his face with his hands. Through his fingers, in a muffled voice, he said, "I am *so* confused."

Walt had stood there the whole time listening to the two boys, his head continuing to twitch every so often. "What do you need to know, Gilbert? I can explain most of it. If the program in my brain allows me to."

Gilbert dropped his hands and gripped the edge of the bar. "*You* are a robot?" he said in almost a whisper.

"Yes. Once I reached the age of thirty I was converted over. Pete over there," he pointed to a man at the table playing cards, "won the lottery and was converted before me. Lucky fellow!" Twitch.

Gilbert had turned around in his seat to see the man Walt was speaking of. The guy was knocking back a large can of oil. The black liquid oozed into his mouth. Screwing his face up in disgust, Gilbert faced the bartender again. "D-Do you remember anything before you were converted?" Gilbert stammered.

Walt pressed his lips together, rolling his eyes to the side, thinking. Then: "Not really. My memory is blank."

"So, you don't know what it was like being a kid?"

"No. According to the Baron, all children are mischievous brats."

"You think that me and Rodney are?"

"Sure." He smiled. Twitched. "All kids are."

"Then, why haven't you turned us in?"

"Turned you into whom?"

"The Baron."

"Oh. Well, I've always liked Rodney's company. And I seem to like yours."

"*Seem* to?"

"Yeah. My robotic brain is still making assumptions whether I should or not. Wait." Walt's eyes left Gilbert and looked at the wall—his head twitched once or twice—and rolled in their sockets. Gilbert's stomach soured. If the answer was "no," what would happen to him?

When Walt's eyes returned to being normal, not jittery, he said: "My brain informed me that I am to like you, too."

"I would hope so. What if you didn't?"

"I would have to kill you on the spot for escaping prison."

"How lucky I am," Gilbert said as he felt a shroud of gloom cover him like a blanket.

From behind them a voice boomed, interrupting the conversation. "Rodney. Gilbert. Please stay seated while we place metal handcuffs on you. Under the rules written in the *Book of Bloth*, law number 128-H, we are to return you to the prison."

Gilbert twisted around and saw two armed guards standing in the doorway.

And gasped.

* * * *

"Stay where you are," one of the guards said with his rifle raised.

Gilbert looked at Rodney. "What do we do now?"

"I don't know. Go back, I guess."

"Won't they kill us for escaping?"

"Probably. Depends."

"Depends on what?"

"How nice Judge Horace is today. If he's in a good mood, he'll let us live and allow us to go back to our cell. If not, well..." Rodney said and shrugged his shoulders, "we may die."

"You mean we have to go back and face the judge again?"

"Yep. Standard procedure, you know. Been there, done that."

"I thought you said you were never caught outside the prison!"

"I never told you that I wasn't caught. Only that I like to go for a stroll."

"Rodney," Gilbert shook his head, "you're killing me!"

Rodney tilted his head. "I'm not killing you. What are you talking about?"

"I'm saying," Gilbert's voice rose in frustration, "you are driving me nuts! Getting on my nerves!"

For a moment Rodney's face looked sad. He sniffled.

Gilbert suddenly felt bad. "Look, Rodney, I'm sorry. Okay? I'm just rattled a bit. I don't want to die."

Rodney wiped a tear out of his eye. "Oh, I know you didn't mean what you said." He smiled.

"Convict Rodney and Convict Gilbert, you are to return with us." The guards stepped forward, handcuffs dangling in one of the guard's hands.

Unexpectedly, one of the men at the table playing cards stood up, knocking over the chair he was sitting in, and started convulsing like someone who had just gotten filled with lead by a machine gun. The cowboy hat he wore fell off. His eyes rolled sideways in their sockets and slid up into his head, showing only his whites. His mouth gaped open and his lips quivered.

Oddly, the others who sat at the table continued playing cards as if they were oblivious to what was going on.

"Oh-oh!" Walt said. "Looks like Pete is gonna need a re-charge. His battery is dying quick!"

Poor Pete stumbled backwards into both of the guards, making them lose their balance. The handcuffs slipped from the one guard's grip—as well as each of their rifles.

Gilbert noticed and shouted, "We need to move, Rodney!"

"Yep. Let's get outta here!"

"Use that door, boys!" Walt pointed to a wooden door off to the side. "It goes out into the alley."

"Thanks," Gilbert said and led the way, twisting open the doorknob and stepping out into the alley.

Soon the boys sprinted down the dusty street. Shortly after, they heard shots reverberate off the shops that lined the street.

At first, when Gilbert glanced back, he thought he would see both of the guards standing there, the rifles pointed at him and Rodney. But that wasn't the case. No one stood in the street.

Before he could ask where the shots came from, Rodney explained, in between breaths. "I bet...they...just shot and killed...Walt!"

"The guards would do that? Shoot other robots?"

"Yep. Walt helped us... Aiding and imbedding fugitives. According to the *Book*...the *Book of Bloth*, anyone— or...robot—who helps convicted felons...is...to be shot...on the...spot!"

"That's terrible!"

"That's the rules."

Another few shots thundered as the boys curved around a

shop and headed for another woodland area.

"Who did they shoot now?" Gilbert asked.

"Probably the other two…robots that were…in the bar."

Gilbert thought a minute. He had counted a total of six, including Walt. "Two robots? I thought there was more than that?"

Rodney stopped, caught his breath, placed a hand on a huge tree. "The guy who stood up at the table was a robot. The others at the card table were only holograms."

"Holograms?"

"You know, a three-dimensional image reproduced from a pattern of interference produced by a split coherent beam of radiation."

Shocked at Rodney's sudden burst of vocabulary and proper definition of the word, Gilbert said, "Um. I know what it means, Rodney—well, repeating the definition of it like you just did, I couldn't do that—but those robots weren't really sitting there?"

"Nope. They weren't even robots. Only holograms. It was a live computer game that someone could play."

"Even a robot?"

"Yep."

"That's weird."

"Not really."

"It is to me!"

Rodney turned to go into the woods, and Gilbert asked, "What other robot was in there to be killed?"

Without turning to face Gilbert, Rodney responded with: "The piano player."

"But if you think about it," Gilbert said, "neither that robot, or the other robot, really had anything to do with helping us."

"No. The guards only assumed it."

"Only assumed it? They shot them on sight, just like that?"

"Yep."

"I guess they were in the wrong place at the wrong time."

"That's a good way to put it, Gilbert."

Both boys ventured into the darkness of the woods with the hopes of eluding the guards for good. After a while, Gilbert asked, "Do all of the robots actually have batteries that have to be recharged every so often?"

"Yep. They have a docking station close by to recharge."

"Where?"

"There are some inside the shops back in the town."

"Oh. What do they look like?"

"Um. I'll have to show you if we see one. Kinda hard to explain."

"Okay." Gilbert glanced over his shoulder, and the town had disappeared from view—they were already deep into the woods. Above, the moon beamed its silver glow. All around them, the nightly creatures spoke, and Gilbert wondered if they were made of flesh and bone—or robotic.

The woods began to darken as the branches of the trees blocked out the shine of the moon and brought forth the feeling of dread inside both boys' stomachs. A fear of being lost in the woods forever played over and over in Gilbert's brain.

And the scary books he had read in the past did not help matters.

"Rodney? Where are we at?"

"Don't know. Never been this far out."

"Oh. That's right." Gilbert had forgotten that they were blind to the fact of what lay ahead.

They walked over dead leaves, making sounds like the cracking of bones. To Gilbert it was as if the woods loomed around him and pressed darkness into his vision. However, traveling a bit farther, over a small hill, brought them in front of a ten-foot-high metal pyramid with a door. Red lights were lined across the top, winking off and on.

"What the heck is that?" Gilbert asked.

"I think it's an entrance to the next Sector."

"Like, Sector Four?"

"Yep. Since we are in Sector Three."

"Now, what about Sectors One and Two? Are there robots there, too?"

"Don't know. No one has ever told me that."

"Have you asked?"

"Once or twice. No one seems to know."

"Or, if they do know, they aren't saying, right?"

Rodney shrugged. "Hard to say, Gilbert."

"Well. What do we do now? Go through this thing?"

"I guess."

Without much of a warning, a solid choice was made for them. A bright spotlight speared their bodies, and a voice thundered: "*Brgggggttt!* STOP! UNDER BARON LAW

YOU ARE UNDER ARREST AND MUST BE DETAINED
AND TAKEN BACK TO PRISON!"

They shielded their eyes, trying to see who—or what—
lay behind the glare. Gilbert wondered if it could be the same
machine that had been in the courtroom. Funny that it would
be all the way out here, he thought; however, the way Gilbert's luck was going and the way this world has already
shown him how odd it was, anything was possible.

"Gilbert! Follow me!" Rodney snapped.

"Into that portal?"

"Yep!"

Rodney punched a few buttons on a keypad and, at first, the
doors refused to open. He tried again, without much luck.

"C'mon, Rodney! Hurry up!"

"I'm tryin'!"

"STAY WHERE YOU ARE, HUMANS. *Brgggtttt!* DO
NOT TRY AND ESCAPE. I AM INSTRUCTED TO SHOOT
ON SIGHT."

The words did not quite sit well in Gilbert's gut. "Hurry
up!" he shouted.

"I said I'm tryin'!" Rodney punched more buttons, over
and over, sometimes hammering on them with his fist.

There was a pop, something moved, and something fell
into place behind the blazing light. "MY WEAPONS ARE
ARMED. I WILL SHOOT IN TEN SECONDS. TEN…" It
started counting down.

Gilbert felt as if the end of his life was coming crashing
down. He did not want to die. He wanted to find Bobby. He

wanted his mom. He wanted his dad. And, most of all, he wanted to get away from this terrible world of terror!

"NINE."

"Rodney! C'mon, dude!"

Gilbert saw the horror across Rodney's face as he snatched a quick glance over his shoulder, then went back to punching numbers on the keypad. Over and over he tried, but the door held fast, like it was some metal troll with its arms folded across its massive chest who would not allow anyone to pass. No matter what.

"EIGHT."

"We're. Gonna. Die. Rodney!" Gilbert screamed, the cords on his neck standing out.

"SEVEN."

Lines of sweat cascaded down Rodney's cheeks, and his eyes bugged out of their sockets while his finger flew.

"SIX."

Gilbert scanned the ground for a branch or something that might bust the door open.

"FIVE."

A long, twisted branch lay off to the side. He ran to it.

"FOUR."

Gilbert placed his hands on it, tried to lift it.

"THREE."

And it was like lifting an anvil.

"TWO."

The door slid apart, revealing sunlight.

"ONE."

Gilbert saw it, rushed through, following a frantic Rodney.

Before the doors closed, a shot slipped through and hit a tree, setting it on fire. The top half tipped backward, broke off, and slammed the ground. Hard.

As the metal doors shut out the horror, Gilbert and Rodney lay sprawled out on the ground. They looked over at each other. Each boy dripped sweat and fear.

"That. Was. *Close!*" Gilbert said.

"Yep," Rodney said, out of breath.

A large shadow fell over the two, and the barrel of a shotgun nuzzled Gilbert's shoulder.

"If you value your young lives," a low, hoarse voice spoke, "do not move."

* * * *

"What are you doing here?" The voice was quick, to the point.

The two didn't reply, sat there not moving a muscle.

"I said," the gun cocked, "what are you boys doing here?"

"We just came through that door."

"I saw that. I didn't ask where you came from. I asked what you are doing here!"

"Escaping prison, sir," Rodney said.

The one behind Gilbert moved. There was a *smack!* and Rodney let loose a cry. "Don't hit me!"

"I didn't ask you, retard!"

"Leave him alone!" Gilbert turned his head only a fraction before the voice told him to keep his eyes straight ahead or pay the same price as his friend had. He followed the rules, but with a growing anger in his chest.

"Now," the rude presence returned behind Gilbert, "let's start again... What are you two doing here?"

"Like my friend just tried to tell you, we escaped from prison and are now being hunted down."

Laughter. "Well well. So, I've got me a couple of runaways, huh?"

"We are escapees, sir," Rodney said.

The presence shifted again, and there was another *smack!* Rodney cried out, a sob in tow.

"I said leave him al—"

"Kid, you aren't in any position to make demands. If I were you, I'd keep that hole under your nose shut tight. That goes for you too, retard!"

A silence hung in the air for a few moments. Gilbert very much wanted to reach out and knock the head off of this mean individual, whoever he was. But he knew he could not, not with the possibility of getting shot. And being only a kid didn't help.

Laughter again. "Boy, I can smell a cannibal a mile away. And whatever *you* are." A boot nudged the middle of Gilbert's back. "Get up. Both of you. Now!"

The boys rose. Without turning his head, Gilbert glanced over at Rodney. He had to choke back a few words. The side of his friend's head was bleeding.

"Walk, you two. Left foot first, right foot second."

Gilbert followed the instructions and heard a grunt. Rodney fell down beside him.

"Get up and try it again, retard! Left foot first. Right foot second! See? Your friend there knows how to do it. It ain't that hard!"

Gilbert was told to stop so Rodney could rise and try it again. Rodney followed the instructions to the T this time, and soon they were walking through the woods. Gilbert wondered if this meant his and Rodney's doom.

Above, the sun beat down, warming their bodies. The woods looked normal to Gilbert, much like where he was originally from. Birds could be heard up high, singing, perhaps sitting along the branches; but, because of the leaves, they were blocked from view.

Just ahead lay a cabin. The weather over the years had caused havoc on the outside of its wooden frame, making it look rundown, decayed. The two wooden columns that held up the overhang over the front porch looked as if they strained to keep it from collapsing. One of the four shutters that hung on each side of the two windows leaned to the side, nearly falling off. Behind the house, there was a bark.

"Up those steps," the voice instructed. "But not you, retard. You stay put!"

Gilbert walked up the wooden steps and through the front door. The inside wasn't much more pleasant than the outside, repeating the decay. A kitchen sat off in one corner of the room, with empty cans of soup and vegetables strewn on the floor and dirty dishes piled in the sink. In another corner a fireplace sat tucked into the wall where a few embers had been left over. And a couch, a chair, and a footrest that should have been thrown out years ago with yellow stuffing exposed, sticking out of the wounds of the fabric, sat in the middle of a wooden floor.

"Have a seat. I'll be back. If you run, I'll blow your feet off."

Gilbert nodded and found a seat on the smelly, decrepit couch. When he heard the screen door whine shut, he looked over his shoulder. Not being able to view anything, the only sound he heard was: "Get your tail movin', boy! Go directly into that shed back there!"

Gilbert had no idea what was in store for him or his friend. Dread eased under his flesh. Sitting there, he scanned the room with the hope of finding something to fight with. Something that might be of use. The only thing he could think of was to get up and go into the kitchen and see if there was a knife in one of the drawers. Something long. Something sharp.

But then he thought: Why bring a knife to a gunfight? That guy would shoot me dead!

From outside came a few muffled words and the sliding of a metal door closed with a bang. Seconds later footsteps fell on the wooden steps, the screen door opened, and stepping into Gilbert's eyesight was a tall man looking down at him, wearing bib overalls with long, scraggly black hair.

The man's dark-skinned face scowled. The grip on his shotgun tightened. He said, "Think you boys can go trespassing on my property, huh?"

Gilbert opened his mouth to speak.

"I did not ask you to answer!" his voice boomed. "I'm only stating a fact. I'm keeping your friend out in my shed, locked up. Since you aren't a retard, I can talk to you and you'll understand my words."

Gilbert wanted to tell this guy that Rodney was probably smarter than him. But he didn't push it.

The tall man walked into the kitchen, grabbed a dirty cup, picked up a chrome pot, and poured some coffee. Holding the cup, he walked back over to Gilbert and sat down across from him and placed his gun over his legs. "Now. What is going to happen is this: I'm contacting the Baron to get a reward for finding you. I'm sure the money will be good. I'll be able to fix this old place up." He took a swallow of coffee. "For your friend out there," he motioned over his shoulder with his thumb, "he's goin' to the carnival."

"Carnival?"

The man tensed, holding his cup less than an inch from his lips. His eyes flicked upwards. "The carnival where all of the Freaks go. Zombies. Ghouls. Vampires. A Carnival of the Bizarre. Retards who like to eat human flesh." He smiled, drained his cup, and rose back up to get some more.

This didn't sit well at all with Gilbert. He had no idea how to save Rodney now.

The man came back, stood over him, one hand holding the firearm. "But before I turn you in, I think I'm gonna make you do some cleanin' around here. Hell, maybe I won't turn your butt in and I'll keep you all to myself." He chuckled. "Sometimes a man needs some company. Gets mighty lonely out here in the woods."

Fear slithered down Gilbert's spine.

The man's humor wiped clean off his face. "While I fig-ure out if I'm gonna turn you in or not, you need to get to cleaning. Go out there and feed my wolf. Get the laundry off the line. Come back inside. Exactly in that order. Under-stand?"

"Yes, sir." Gilbert rose and walked to the door.

From behind him the man's voice said, "Don't get any ideas about runnin' off. I'm gonna sit right here and watch you with both of my barrels trained on your feet. If the blast doesn't take you out, I'll release my wolf and he'll eat you alive."

Gilbert gasped and stepped outside. The metal shed sat about ten feet or so from the back porch. He wondered if the guy had hit Rodney again before throwing him into it. If he had, it didn't set very well in his gut. But, really, what could he do about it?

Gilbert focused on a huge gray and white wolf in a large cage. The animal's green eyes stared coldly at Gilbert.

"Where's your wolf's food?" Gilbert shouted.

Out of the kitchen window came: "See that wooden chest sittin' on the ground butted against the cabin?"

"Yeah."

"Open it up and you'll find a dog dish on top of the food. Use it to scoop up the feed and take it to him."

Still looking at the window, Gilbert tried to see the two barrels of the shotgun. He couldn't tell if the gun was pointed at him or not. So, he walked over and flipped open the wooden lid and saw a huge amount of dog food and the dish on top. He did what he was told and cautiously stepped over to the wolf, now having a full dish in hand.

The wolf barked, restlessly moving back and forth in the cage. Its tail did not wag. Its green eyes stared at Gilbert as if it were trying to decide whether it was hungry for food—or him. Of course, Gilbert hoped it was the former, rather than the latter.

Gilbert stopped. He had no idea how to get the food into the cage so the vicious animal could eat.

As if answering his question telepathically, the man's voice barked: "There's a small door to the cage. See it?"

Noticing it, he nodded.

"Slide over the latch and stick the food in there."

Gilbert saw something missing. "What about water? I don't see any?"

"He's already drunk once today. He'll get more when I say so."

Gilbert found that rather odd. He had always known that your pets needed a full bowl of water all of the time. You didn't want them to dehydrate. Unless of course this creature was a robot. Maybe this mean dude was one, too. No— Gilbert shoved the thought aside—if the wolf was robotic, it wouldn't eat. And the animal's owner couldn't be a robot, because he had some serious body odor.

He closed in the gap between him and the caged wolf. The wolf backed away, pressing its hind end against the inside of the cage. It had ceased barking, but growled. As quick as he could Gilbert opened the door, stuck the dish in, closed it, and hurried backward.

The wolf peered up at him, not moving.

"Go ahead and eat, boy. If you don't, your owner may shoot me."

The wolf hesitated a few more seconds, turned its snout toward the metal shed where Rodney was, then focused on the food and stepped over to eat. Muffled, crunching sounds filled the air.

"Get the laundry off the line, boy. Get back inside!"

The man's voice propelled Gilbert forward. He did what he was told by pulling the clothes down and, seeing a basket on the ground, dropped them into it. Two white shirts, a pair of bib overalls, two pairs of briefs with holes in the crotch and two pairs of socks, each with a hole in the toe, lay in the pile.

"Bring them in here and fix me some food. Haven't eaten since breakfast."

Gilbert turned to go and heard the cage rattle. When he looked back he saw the wolf staring at him with one paw pressing on the metal wire. The dish was empty.

"Still hungry?" Gilbert asked.

The wolf cocked its head, as if listening.

"Get in here! Don't talk to my wolf!" The man's voice boomed, and Gilbert rushed inside the back door of the cabin like someone had lit fire to his butt.

* * * *

Night fell, a blanket of darkness. Light from the fire in

the fireplace threw dancing shadows on the cabin's walls. Gilbert had opened a few cans, naked of the labels, by using the pull tabs on top and scooped out what looked to be roast beef in gravy with a metal spoon onto a plate. The man had refused to have it heated.

Sitting in the chair by the fire, the man said, "Get yourself a can of food and eat."

Gilbert finished the dishes and grabbed a clean bowl out of the strainer.

"What the hell are you doing?"

"Grabbing a clean bowl."

"Nonsense! Use mine!" He threw it and nearly hit Gilbert in the face. "We don't need to dirty up another bowl!"

Gilbert reached down and picked up the bowl. Before reaching for a spoon in the drawer, he asked, "What about a sp—"

The spoon sailed past him and bounced off the window and fell to the floor. Gilbert reached down and picked that up, also. He started to hold it under the faucet in the kitchen sink to wash it, but—

"What are you doing?"

"I'm cleaning the spoon first."

"Why?"

"Because you used it and it hit the floor."

"Think I've got a disease or something?"

"No. It's just that it's dirt—"

The man rose. "What's wrong?" His voice was cold.

"It's j-just that it was dirty."

"Well," he stepped over to Gilbert, looming over him, "I ain't got any germs or diseases. Since you've cleaned this floor, it should be good enough to eat off of, right?"

"Um. I don't know."

"You don't know?"

"N-No."

"Well, tell ya what, boy." He licked his lips. "Give me that spoon."

Gilbert handed it over. He winced, thinking the man was going to hit him with it. Instead, all he did was open the back door and throw it outside.

"Since you think I have germs"—he grabbed the can, slipped a spoon out of the drawer, opened it with the pull-tab, and scooped out the food, letting it drop on the floor in a small clump—"you can eat off the floor."

Gilbert looked down. The texture of the food looked disgusting.

"Eat," he pointed, "down on the floor. Now!"

Gilbert slowly bent down and used a finger to scoop up a chunk of it. He placed it between his lips and he nearly gagged.

"What's wrong? Taste bad?" The man chuckled.

Gilbert screwed his face up. The aftertaste was worse than the initial one.

"Well, it should be. It's dog food."

Gilbert's stomach flip-flopped, and the food wanted to crawl back up his throat.

"You'll eat that or not eat at all!" He laughed and walked

back to his chair and sat down.

Gilbert looked down at the food. He didn't think that he could muster the thoughts of placing any more in his mouth. If he threw it up, would the man laugh or knock him across the room?

"What are you waiting for? Eat it, boy!" The man's face turned toward Gilbert, twisted in a scowl. "If you don't eat it, you won't keep your strength up. There's an awful lot to do around here, and I need a slave that'll do the work. That's right. I can tell by the look in your eyes what the word 'slave' means. Don't think I'll give you up to the Baron. Mebbe I'll just keep you for myself. How'd you like that, boy?"

Gilbert only sat there on the floor like a mangy mutt, not replying. Even the smell of the food was turning his stomach.

A smile spread under the man's nose. "Thought you'd like that. Come here a minute."

At first Gilbert didn't budge, but he thought the better of it, and now stood by the man. A large hand reached out and, with a dirty thumb and two fingers with dirt under the fingernails, grabbed his chin and moved his head to the left and right. "Yeah. You are a young one. You'll do just fine. You'll do the work I tell you to do or I'll plug two holes in your friend's head. One bullet to kill him; the other to make sure he's dead." The thumb and fingers let loose. "Now go over there and eat your food. Then over to the corner to get some sleep. Tomorrow the Ringmaster will arrive and take your friend where he needs to go. From then on, your life is mine." The last word was drawn out, suspended in the air.

Gilbert obeyed, somehow eating the disgusting food without hurling it back up, and laid down on the cold, dirty wooden floor minus a blanket or pillow.

Lying there, he wished so much to leave this cabin.

And wished he could make this man pay for his actions.

* * * *

Sunlight speared Gilbert in his eyes. When he woke, the cabin was empty of the mean dude. He rose, stretched, and got up and walked over to the kitchen window. Outside, the man was bent down speaking to his wolf. The animal was pressed against the back of the cage, away from the man, glaring at him.

If the abusive treatment Gilbert received from the man was the same toward the wolf, it would explain the animal's actions.

The man got up. Before he turned around, Gilbert stepped away from the window and hurried back to the corner. No sooner than he had, the back door opened and the man stepped inside.

"Hey. Finally awake," he said. "Think you were gonna sleep all morning long?"

"Um. No, I'm getting up."

"Darn right you are. Work is to be done. A lot to do today." He paused. "Not that it really matters, but what's your name?"

"Gilbert."

"Funny name."

"So I've been told."

"Smartin' off to me, boy?"

"No. I was only saying the same thing I've been saying all d—"

"Words like that will get you knocked across the room." Gilbert's explanation, obviously, did nothing for his situation. "All right. *Gilbert*. You choke down some food and meet me outside."

Gilbert wondered if he could choke down the same food he was given last night to eat. Or not. Before he could think of an answer to the decision, it was made for him, as the man opened another can naked of its label.

"Eat it and meet me outside," he repeated his demand and left the can on the counter, not dumping it out on the floor.

Gilbert got on his feet and retrieved the can. Definitely applesauce. He looked in the sink and in the strainer.

"What are you looking for, boy?" the man said, halfway out the back door.

"A spoon." The word slipped out of Gilbert's mouth before he could stop it.

"Oh. Need a spoon again? Wanna go through what happened last night?"

"Um. No."

"Good. Eat it with your fingers and make it quick. Holes don't dig themselves." The man left, letting the screen door whine shut.

After scooping out as much applesauce as he could without cutting his finger on the rim of the can, Gilbert went outside. He noticed that his stomach growled. He needed more food.

"Over here!" the man shouted. He stood there with a shovel.

Gilbert looked at the metal shed, wondering if this guy had fed his friend or not.

"Quit looking at my shed! That is none of your concern! Get over here. I will not ask again!"

Gilbert hurriedly walked over and stood by the guy.

"Now," the man began, "I want you to dig a deep hole." He handed over the shovel, and Gilbert took it. "And make it about four feet deep and five feet wide all the way around. Got it?"

"Yeah. But I'm not good at math."

"Not my problem. You should have paid better attention in that prison. Shouldn't have slept through your classes."

Gilbert wondered if he was referring to being taught English, science, math, and so forth. Besides locking up kids, did they actually *teach* them too?

"What are you waiting for?"

"Huh?" Gilbert had zoned out.

"I said, 'What are you waiting for?' Get to it!"

"Okay," Gilbert said and stuck the blade into the dirt, shoveling up a chunk and revealing a few worms wiggling out of the bottom. He threw it to the side. Behind him, the back door whined shut.

After shoveling two more huge chunks of earth—or Hearth—he felt eyes on him. Thinking it could be the man standing there hovering over him, gripping his shotgun like a prison guard, he took a chance and glanced over his shoulder.

The wolf sat there in the cage staring, its mouth open, the tongue hanging out.

"Hey, boy. Guess it's a good thing you don't have to do this, huh? 'Cause it sucks."

The wolf only stared.

Gilbert wiped sweat off his brow and he wanted to call out to Rodney, ask if he was doing okay. Taking a chance, though, could result in a beating or much worse. Why didn't he listen to his parents when they asked him to promise not go into that house? He could have been sitting at home right now eating a good meal or out riding his bike. Thoughts of Bobby also slid into his brain. He needed to find him. Maybe Bobby had found a way out and was searching for Gilbert. Maybe. *Just* maybe. If so, Gilbert hoped that Bobby wasn't sitting in prison or somewhere like this, working like a slave, treated badly.

Gilbert's hands began to hurt. He stopped working and noticed he had blisters forming in his palms. Luckily, the hole was nearly done. Thoughts about his parents and Bobby and the terrible situation he was in gave him the drive, perhaps an anger, to get the job completely done. He worked like he was a machine. Or, a robot.

"Well," the voice from the man said, "I see you're good for somethin'." He laughed. "Blisters, huh?"

Gilbert didn't reply.

"I've got some cream that'll take care of that. Right now you need to earn it. Finish the hole." The man walked off.

Gilbert continued to dig using his aching hands and didn't

look up until he saw a horse-drawn carriage pull up with the words CARNIVAL OF THE BIZARRE written on the side. The driver was a small, chunky fellow with a top hat on his head. He climbed down and, if he fell, Gilbert wondered if he would bounce.

"How do, how do, boy!" The man's words were spoken quickly, and he was grinning ear to ear.

The back door opened, and Gilbert's tormentor stepped out. "Here for the boy?" the man snapped, pointing to the shed.

"Oh." The chunky man's thick eyebrows rose. "You have *two?*"

"When I notified them, I only said I had one to give." His eyes fell on Gilbert. "This one's mine."

"Oh. Won't the Baron be mad! Yes he will! Yes. He. Will!"

"I'll deal with the Baron. He knows me."

"I'm sure he does, he does. But, my good man, for the right price I can take this specimen off your hands. No trouble made from the Baron, you'll never have. This boy will make a nice addition to my act. Yes, yes, indeedy!"

"I said he's mine. Not for sale."

"Oh, let me tell you my good man, I can make a price that you cannot refuse!"

"I'm refusing. I'll get you the other one. Then you can get off my property."

"But let us go inside and talk about this. Brew some tea?"

"I don't drink tea."

"Brew some hot cocoa? Surely you wouldn't turn down a

cup of chocolate?" The plump man tipped back and forth on his heels with his hands behind his back and his face beaming.

"I don't drink hot cocoa."

"Well, what about—"

"Getting off my land before I tear your face off."

A long pause hung in the air before the plump little man spoke again. "Well. You don't have to be mean about it. All you had to do was say you weren't interested."

The man grumbled, shook his head. "There is nothing more to talk about." He walked over and unlocked the shed's doors and slid them open. "Get outta there, freak!"

At first Gilbert wondered what he would see. Would Rodney be malnourished? Thin? No. As he emerged he was the same old Rodney that Gilbert knew. But with a face twisted in fear. When he saw Gilbert, he smiled.

Gilbert returned the gesture and saw that the wound on the side of his friend's head had healed up.

"Get him outta here. Now!" the tall man raged.

"Y-Yes, yes, I will." The plump guy wobbled over and opened the carriage's wooden door. "Get in the back there, boy. That's right. Sit right there. Good." He closed and padlocked it and began climbing back up to the seat.

"Hey! Where's my money? Skimping out on Gerald?"

"Oh. No, no, my good man. So sorry, Gerald. So, sorry." He climbed back down, reached into his front pocket and pulled out a pack of greenish-blue bills and handed them over. Gerald counted them.

"Now. I must go. My show awaits me, and my newly acclaimed friend in the coach." The guy climbed back up, and the horse began moving.

"Good evening to all, and to all a good night!" the plump guy shouted.

Gilbert watched Rodney as he waved 'bye and the horse-drawn carriage drew away, swallowed by the woods.

"You ain't done yet. Get to workin', boy!" Gerald barked.

Gilbert started back and his blisters popped, oozing. He wandered if that guy had been the Ringmaster.

* * * *

Right before sunset Gilbert dug the hole the best he could, making it nearly precise to Gerald's specs. Since he'd been told that his height was four feet seven inches tall, he was able to check how deep he had dug every so often by standing up straight and seeing how much of his head poked out. The width and length looked good. He hoped.

"Time to eat," Gerald barked out of the kitchen window.

Gilbert's body felt miserable. His hands hurt him terribly, and his mouth was dry. Slowly, he staggered up to the screen door and entered inside. On the counter was an open can and, as usual, it was missing a label.

"Eat." Gerald had already sat down in front of the lit fireplace. "Then go out and feed my wolf. Don't stay out there very long—you'll need to get back in here and get some rest. You'll need your strength for tomorrow."

Tomorrow? What am I going to have to do next? I feel horrible!
After choking down small chunks of beef soaked in gravy—

bitter, slimy food—he went outside.

The wolf was lying down. When it saw Gilbert, its head rose.

Gilbert retrieved the food from the wooden chest, walked to the cage and went to open the small door, but it was stuck. He pulled on it and it did not open. He glanced over his shoulder, thinking that if he didn't hurry and feed Gerald's pet, he may get punished. Though, as bad as he felt, he would probably be too numb to feel anything.

He tried to pull the door open again without any luck.

Then he saw the bigger door and figured he could slip the food in that way. He hoped.

The wolf eyed him.

"Please don't attack me. This is the only way I can get you any food." Cautiously, he opened the door, placed the food inside. This time the wolf did not back up against the cage. It sat up.

Gilbert glanced over his shoulder and looked back at the wolf. "Go ahead and eat, boy."

The wolf cocked his head.

"Go ahead, now."

The wolf turned its head toward the house and then back at Gilbert, letting loose a low growl.

Gilbert froze. He suddenly noticed that he was farther inside than he'd thought. Being really worn out and tired from digging the hole, he hadn't been paying enough attention. Slowly, trying to rectify the situation, he backed away.

The wolf growled louder and stepped forward.

Gilbert swallowed. "Stay right there, boy," he said and motioned with his hands. "Please? So I can get out of here."

The wolf took another step forward with a quick glance toward the kitchen window. Its green eyes came back to Gilbert.

"Please let me get out of the cage. I don't want you to bite m—"

No sooner than Gilbert's feet were out of the cage, the wolf lunged. Gilbert fell back, and all he could see was the large body of the wolf leaping over him, blocking out the full moon hanging high in the night sky. Horrible thoughts of what Gerald was going to do to him now filtered through his mind. And the results did not look pretty.

Quickly, Gilbert rose and started off toward the woods. Maybe he could find a way to escape from this horror. Maybe he would be lucky enough to find Bobby and discover the nearest door back to his world.

But that didn't happen. What did happen was a crash through the screen door behind him. A vision of Gerald standing there with the shotgun pointed at his back slid under the top of his skull. Fear of what would happen next, perhaps a very harsh punishment, came to his mind.

When he turned to face the Reaper, he only saw the huge hole in the screen door where the wolf had leapt through. From inside, Gerald hollered out a few words before there was another crash and a roar.

"Get away from me! I'll blow you to Kingdom Come, Wendell!"

There was a shotgun blast and a roar burst through the kitchen's open window, bouncing off the woods.

Gilbert's bowels nearly drained.

Another shotgun blast. The roar came again, drowning out Gerald's cries, soon followed by silence. All he heard now was normal nighttime sounds.

Gilbert froze. He wasn't sure what to think. He sure as heck didn't know if he should run or not.

Stepping out of the cabin was a tall, stocky silhouette with green eyes glowing. One minute the figure did not look human, more canine; the next he definitely appeared human. In his right hand he carried the shotgun.

Gilbert backed away, nearly losing his balance. And before he knew it, the shadow of the tall figure stood over him. The eyes were no longer glowing green, and the man bent down on one knee.

"You okay, Gilbert?" he asked.

"Um. Yeah. Guess so."

The guy smiled. "I'm Wendell." He held out his hand.

Gilbert's eyes fixated on the shotgun.

"Oh. Don't worry about this thing." Wendell laid it down. "I'm not gonna shoot you."

Cautiously, Gilbert shook Wendell's hand. The guy's palm was hairy, and it tickled his. Gilbert winced when Wendell squeezed. The blisters were still there.

"Are you okay? Did my brother harm you?"

Brother? "No. I'm fine." Gilbert rubbed his hand with the other.

"Your hand okay? Did I squeeze it too hard?"

"No. It's fine. Just got some blisters from digging that hole over there."

"Hang on a second and I'll get you some lotion to put on it." Wendell left Gilbert standing outside and returned within minutes, holding a jar. "I want to thank you for letting me out of that cage." He unscrewed the lid. "If it hadn't been for you, I'd still be in there."

"I, uh, didn't let you out. I only left the cage's door open, and you jumped over me."

"Oh," he chuckled, "sorry about that. Guess you're right. But you did allow me to escape. Here, use two fingers and scoop out some of this. Good. Now rub it in."

Gilbert screwed up his face. "Stuff stinks!"

"I know, but it does its work. You'll notice it pretty quick."

And Gilbert did. His palms were almost back to normal and not aching one bit.

"Sorry, I didn't mean to scare you. I had a bone to pick with Gerald." His expression darkened, and he glared at the empty cage. "He placed me in that cage and rubbed wolfsbane all over it, preventing me from escaping. I found the jar and dumped it all around him. When he wakes up he's in for a surprise."

Gilbert glanced at the cabin. "So, he's not dead?"

"No." Wendell sat the jar down on the ground. "Only knocked out. He'll be awake before long, so we need to get."

Gilbert nodded. "Won't he be trapped with the,

the…did you say wolfsbane?"

"Yep. He won't be for long. He has a way of getting in and out of trouble. Always had. Even when he and I were cubs. We do need to get as far away from this place as possible, Gilbert. I suppose we need to find your friend, too."

"Rodney?"

"The one," Wendell pointed to the shed, "whom Gerald kept in there."

"Yeah, that's Rodney. I think they took him to a circus."

"They usually take cannibals there. Even my kind for their despicable acts."

"Your kind?"

"Well, mine and my brother's."

"Um. What kind is that?"

Wendell cocked his head. "You don't know? Did you not see what happened in the cabin?"

"I only heard it."

"Probably a good thing that you didn't."

"I'm not from around here."

"Kinda sensed that. Where are you from? I thought you and Rodney were escapees from the Baron's prison?"

"Well, we are. But I'm not actually from this world. Or Sector that we're in."

"Mmmph." Wendell scratched his chin. "Where are you from?"

"Another place where there aren't robots and mean judges and guards and cannibals."

119

"Really? Strange. I thought that the Baron owned everything."

"Not where I'm from."

"Huh. Learn something new every day. Well, c'mon, Gilbert, we need to find your friend and get him away from the Ringmaster."

"That was that guy's name?"

"Which guy?"

"The one who took Rodney."

"That's Tilbit."

"Oh." Instead of pursuing Tilbit's relationship with the Ringmaster, Gilbert asked, "What will the Ringmaster do to Rodney?"

"Nothing good. The guy calls people like us freaks of nature and wants to keep us in cages. And you already know how much I like being caged."

Gilbert nodded, then asked, "People like you?"

"Yep. Werewolves." Wendell grinned and showed his teeth, which were not jagged at the moment.

Gilbert's stomach knotted up and his body tensed. First cannibals, now were (*gulp!*) wolves?

"Oh. Don't be scared, Gilbert! I'm not going to harm you! You helped me. Now, I'm helping you."

Gilbert relaxed.

"See, you have to understand the history between me and my brother. We have never liked each other. He's very mean. And whenever I saw him shouting at you, anger grew inside me."

"He was mean! He made me eat dog food and clean and

dig that hole over there!" Gilbert pointed.

Wendell licked his lips. "Do you know why he made you do that?"

"No."

"That was going to be your grave. He was going to eventually kill you."

Gilbert was silent for a few seconds before he spoke again. "Why would he kill me?"

"Because he hates Abnormals like you."

"Abnormals?"

"Humans who aren't cursed like werewolves, cannibals, zombies, or vampires, or even robots. They're nearly extinct here."

"Say what? There aren't many people who are human? There's mostly vampires and zombies?"

"Yep. See, my brother Gerald has always been a mean one, Gilbert. Ran with the wrong pack growing up."

"So, are there any robots in this Sector?"

"A few. The Ringmaster is one. Others are only servants. See, the Baron sectioned us off in this world to live. He calls us Freaks. The Ringmaster is sort of a thorn in our side, thanks to the Baron. And when I say *our*, I mean my kind, the vampires, the zombies, and the cannibals."

"As much as I've heard about this Baron, I would have figured he would have already turned you into robots."

"Nope. He's actually afraid of us. 'Course, he won't admit it." Wendell sniffed, rubbed his nose. "Our breed, like the vampire, go back a long way. Even before the Baron was born."

"Wow!"

"Hey. We need to move. My brother will be up soon."

"Okay." A part of Gilbert wished that Gerald would never wake up and would die instead. Then he felt bad for thinking such a thing.

"Follow me. I know these woods like the pentagram in the palm of my hand."

"Okay."

And off Gilbert went, leaving the bad taste of Gerald and his cabin behind.

* * * *

The moon shone down on Gilbert as he followed his new friend through the woods. Slivers of moonlight railed through the trees, hitting the ground.

"So, you know where Rodney will be?"

"I can find him by his scent. The Ringmaster doesn't stay in one town very long; no more than a few days."

"What's this circus like, Wendell? Does the Ringmaster torture vampires and zombies and werewolves? Is he a human or what?"

"The Ringmaster, like I said, is a robot and so are his workers."

"Oh. That's right. Forgot you said it."

"No problem. He makes the Freaks do what he says or they get a silver bullet in a limb or a stake through the heart."

Gilbert thought for minute, then asked, "What about the zombies? He can't torture or maybe even kill what is already dead."

"Sure he can. He takes an axe to them, chopping off their hands and feet if they try and escape. To actually kill them, though, he sets fire to them."

"Wow!" Gilbert said. "Wendell, how come you know so much about this Ringmaster?"

"Let's just say that he and I have a history together. If I get a chance, I've got a bone to pick with him."

Gilbert was sort of afraid to ask exactly what that particular bone might be. So, he stayed quiet.

The woods parted, and the two stepped into a large field. The ground was wet and nearly sucked Gilbert's tennis shoes off his feet. As it was, his feet were instantly soaked.

"Man! My feet are wet!" Gilbert spat.

Wendell glanced back at him and smiled. "Sorry, Gilbert. I guess I should have gotten you some boots back at my brother's cabin, like I'm wearing."

"They probably wouldn't fit. Your brother has big feet. So do you."

Wendell chuckled. "Yeah, I sure do, don't I?"

Gilbert smiled.

The field ended at a wide dirt road, but started again on the other side, running straight into another patch of woods. Wendell stopped, and Gilbert almost bumped into him.

After standing there for a few seconds, sniffing the air, Wendell said, "We'll take this road and go in that direction." He pointed to the west.

"Okay," Gilbert responded.

As they walked Gilbert noticed that the road held deep

ruts in it. He figured they might be caused by wagon wheels.

Trees climbed the sky, blocking out the moon. Somewhere nearby an owl hooted.

"This place looks creepy, Wendell," Gilbert said, trying not to stumble over the ruts in the road.

"Even I agree with you," Wendell said, nearly stumbling over the uneven path. "I hope we don't have to look long to find the carnival."

"Me, too."

Night sounds fluttered in the air, and Gilbert swatted a few mosquitoes that pestered him. Abruptly, the road curved and the two stopped walking. Down below a long hill the carnival was all set up, stabbing the darkness with its multicolored lights, blinking like stars in the sky, feeding a small town with its dreadful delights.

"Down there is the town of Briar, Gilbert. It's mostly made up of ghosts. Stay close, okay?" Wendell looked down at Gilbert. He nodded. "This place isn't for a boy like you. It's very dangerous."

Gilbert did not want to ask anything further about the place. Or the ghosts, for that matter. His encounters with ghosts, so far, had not been a pleasant retreat.

"C'mon, let's go get Rodney," Wendell said.

Gilbert followed the friendly lycanthrope down the hill, and his gut feeling made him wonder if he was stepping into a huge grave.

* * * *

"Come one, come all, to the greatest carnival on the planet!

The best place to see zombies get hacked up and piece themselves back together! A place to see an actual werewolf shot with a silver bullet and live! A place to watch a vampire impaled through the heart with a wooden stake and still live!" A slim figure with a long face, thick eyebrows, a handlebar mustache under his nose and a cape drawn around his shoulders shouted to a captivated ghostly audience while standing atop the same horse-drawn carriage that had taken Rodney away.

Gilbert and Wendell stood behind a huge crowd of ghosts, listening close.

Earlier, entering over the threshold of Briar had only brought silence. At first. Then out of nowhere a male ghost ran across the dusty street while two others chased him, shouting obscenities, holding ghostly hatchets.

Wendell stepped in front of Gilbert, shielding him from the horror. Though, as soon as it had begun, it ended while they watched the ghost slip into the wall of a shop and the other two follow.

"The heck was that?" Gilbert asked, peeking around Wendell.

"Couple of ghosts who must have been in a disagreement about something."

"Like what?"

"Could be the one who was being chased was trying to stay in a house where he was unwanted. He could have trespassed and those other two didn't like it. Ghosts are territorial, Gilbert. They like to stay haunting one spot."

"I've watched programs about people investigating

ghosts. They go in with their detectors and try and talk to them."

"Programs?"

"On television."

Wendell frowned. "Television?"

"Yeah. There's things called shows and movies and cartoons on there for people to watch."

"I've never heard of such a thing."

"It's pretty cool."

"Can you explain it further?"

It was Gilbert's turn to frown. "Well. I guess it's like nourishment for the brain, instead of the stomach."

"Sounds interesting."

"It is."

"So, these people—I'm gonna assume they are human like you—try and find ghosts?"

"Yeah. They try and talk to them."

"Why?"

"'Cause they may haunt a house where someone lives. That someone may not want a ghost in their house."

"I can see why. Especially back in your world. Ghosts are restless."

"I noticed."

Every other ghost in town was in the square at the carnival. As the two continued their travel, Gilbert noticed the town was made up of dilapidated and decrepit-looking shops, bars and a tall hotel that towered over the dusty street. After passing by a few windows lit by candlelight in the hotel, he wondered why he only saw apparitions of women in dresses peeking out of the glass or standing on the balconies. When he looked up at Wendell, opening his mouth to ask, his new friend shook his head. It must have been something bad to talk about. So, he left it at that.

"Do you think we'll be okay around all of these ghosts?" Gilbert whispered through cupped hands at Wendell while the man on the carriage still raved about the show.

Wendell looked down at him. "Yeah. You're safe with me, Gilbert. These ghosts," he pointed, "know my kind, and we're sorta on the same side. Except for a few who aren't; but that's another story. Another time, I can fill you in about. That all right?"

"Yep. That's cool."

"Cool?"

"It means that's fine."

"Oh. Nice word."

Meanwhile, from atop the carriage, the caped announcer beckoned. "How 'bout it, friends? Mmmmm? Anyone interested in seeing the marvel of the planet? Anyone interested in seeing the impossible happen? Mmmmm? How about this: I get to show you a surprise that will make your corpses turn over in their graves! Mmmmm? Yes. I see your tomb-bound faces. I see that you all are very interested. Yes indeed! Here in the carnival, anything is possible! And what more could you ask for when the show is free, free, FREE!"

The ghostly crowd shifted, floating back and forth, as each ghostly figure of a man and woman nodded and smiled.

"Well, then, step through that doorway and feast your ghostly eyes on what lies BEYOND!"

Gilbert had not even noticed the single doorway off to the side, hovering about two feet off the ground in the air all by itself. Standing by it stood none other than the chubby guy who had taken Rodney. A wide grin spread across his face.

"There's Tilbit!" Gilbert snapped.

Wendell nodded. "I see him. The Ringmaster's right-hand man. He's the one you saw there earlier today, collecting Rodney."

"Yep," Gilbert agreed. "So, where's the Ringmaster?"

"Right there on top of the carriage speaking to us." Wendell nodded a second time, toward the slim figure.

"Oh."

The ghosts lined up in a single file and started going through the door as Tilbit stood there, tipping back and forth on his heels. He smiled and smiled as his boss continued to feed the flame about the show to the anxious crowd.

Gilbert and Wendell fell in line behind the ghost of a man in his early twenties. The guy turned around.

"You two visitors in town?"

"Passin' through. That's all," Wendell informed him.

"Mmmph." His eyebrows rose. "Welcome to the ghost town of Briar, then. I hope you have a pleasant stay."

"Do you get very many visitors?" Gilbert asked.

"Not really. Kinda gets a bit lonely here. You two probably already know that, huh?"

Of course, Gilbert did not know much about the guy's

town, and he didn't ask about it either.

"This carnival will be the highlight of our year," the ghost continued. "It's always been for, oh, I would have to say a hundred years or more."

"A hundred years?" Gilbert gasped.

"Or more. It's hard to keep track, being dead, you know. Time passes by so fast. One minute you've been alive for twenty-five years, the next you're killed and converted."

Converted? Like being converted into a robot. He only nodded, not quite knowing what to add to that. Had this guy been a victim under the Baron's brutality?

"Yes, yes, looks like we have a vast crowd tonight," the Ringmaster shouted. "Keep following in a single line inside, please, to feast your ghostly eyes on the spectacle on the planet of Hearth!"

The line crept closer and closer to the doorway, and Gilbert saw that it was only made of wood. Or appeared to be. Each figure floated into the doorway instead of having to make a huge step up. Nothing but the dusty road sat under it. He wondered how that could possibly be because now he could see directly into the doorway, reminding him of the views of booths made of wood. Then he thought about the world he was in. How very odd it was. It was like the impossible had crash-landed here.

"Ever seen this show before, you two?" the ghost asked.

"I have," Wendell said, "long ago. This boy, here, hasn't."

"It is a *sight* to see," the ghost told Gilbert.

They were now beside Tilbit and almost through the

doorway. As the ghostly young man stepped through, the plump little man's eyes fell on Wendell and, at first, he was smiling. Now the expression washed away. "W-Wendell?"

"Hey there, Tilbit. How are you? How's the knee?" Wendell smiled. "Better?"

Tilbit's eyes fell on Gilbert, recognizing him. He switched back to Wendell. "Ah." He cleared his throat. "Much better, thanks. I'm, ah, doing fine. Yes. I'm just fine." He cleared his throat again. "You?"

"Very well, thank you." Wendell glanced at Gilbert. "This here," he introduced, "is Gilbert. You remember him, don't you?"

"Uh, I th-think so." Tilbit pulled on his collar, as if someone had cranked up the heat.

"Oh, I'm sure you do, Tilbit. Your mind hasn't turned senile, has it?"

"Uh. No, Wendell. It hasn't." Tilbit looked a little shocked with a dash of fear.

"Look. We don't want any trouble here. Okay? What we want is Rodney back. Returned unharmed."

"S-Sure. But the only problem with that request is dealing with my boss."

"Oh, I think he can be persuaded, Tilbit."

"If you say so." Tilbit's smile came back, but it wasn't meaningful. Sort of artificial.

"I say so because I know."

A long pause fell between the three until Tilbit broke the silence. "Well, uh," he pulled on his collar again, "go on through. Enjoy the show. Yes. Enjoy the show!"

"Don't worry, we will. Take care of yourself."

"Th-thank you, Wendell. I will."

A few more steps and they entered into the carnival. The scenery on both sides had changed drastically, as they now stood inside of a portal. Booths were lined up on both sides of a dusty street that led straight up to a huge red tent. A small crowd of ghosts observed the games from the booths.

"What's up with Tilbit's knee, Wendell? Did you hurt it?"

"A long time ago he came after me. Back when I was younger, living in a small town, almost like Briar but without ghosts. I think it might have been around the time the carnival started and the Ringmaster was fetching werewolves, vampires and zombies. With Tilbit, I had to make sure he did not think of ever coming after me again. A little something to make him remember to stay away from me." Wendell grinned, showing his canines.

Gilbert did not pry any further.

"Step right up, step right up! Win a prize!" a voice hollered out over everyone. When Gilbert looked to see where it was coming from, he didn't see a sign of anyone.

"Try your luck? Eh? Try your luck and win a prize?"

Now Gilbert noticed it. The voice was coming from a speaker hung above the booth. But where was the speaker himself?

"C'mon, Gilbert, we need to make it to the tent."

Gilbert noticed that each booth had a speaker. Each voice

that came through spoke in different tones, high or low, trying to charm any passerby into playing the games. At one
booth, you could try your luck and throw colored hoops over
cut-off heads of zombies who grinned and bobbed to the left
and to the right; at one booth you had to try and catch the or-
ange-colored snake by its tail as it tried to bite you while it
swam in a loop of water; and other booths had balloons hung
on a wall to try and pop with darts that splattered with blood.
There was even a game where you used a fake rifle on a stand
to shoot small metal shapes of werewolves that ran back and
forth along a track in an artificial forest setting—it had a
strong similarity to the human game of shooting ducks.

Wendell screwed up his face in disgust at the werewolf
game. "Once we are inside, Gilbert, stay close. Not being
from this world, for someone like yourself, the sights in there
may seem very odd."

"And all of this *isn't?*" Gilbert interjected, his finger
pointing at the booth with severed hands running amuck inside a rectangular glass tray. Whatever that game was, he did
not want to find out.

Wendell saw it. "Ahhh." He nodded. "Guess I didn't have
to remind you, huh?"

"Nope."

"Wendell, how come this town is full of only ghosts?"

"Guess I should have explained to you earlier, huh? See,
Gilbert, this town is made up of many different souls. Have
you learned what the Baron does to Abnormals after they turn
thirty?"

"Yep. I read part of the *Book of Bloth*."

"No kiddin'? Where?"

"In a robot town called Basteel. Me and Rodney went there right after we escaped prison."

"Oh. I've heard of that place, I think. Sector Three, right?"

"I think so."

"So, you know that the Baron, um, how shall I say this..."

"It's okay. You can say it. It won't scare me. I know he kills adults because he turns them into robots. He keeps all the children in prison because he thinks we are all brats."

"That is absolutely correct, Gilbert. That Baron is one bad guy. But, back to your original question...the ghosts here are the ones who have died under the Baron's laws. They are the ones who have perished."

"Really? All these ghosts are from the Baron's victims, and now they live in Briar?"

"As far as I know."

"That is really weird!"

"What is weirder is that I've also heard an old zombie tale about a Sector that has nothing but graveyards where some end up, instead of here. I can't prove it because I really don't know if it exists or not."

The thought of a graveyard chilled Gilbert a bit. He never really liked them. In the daylight they were places where one could go and bury their loved ones or visit to mourn the dead. Gilbert had never heard of someone going there at night to mourn, since they were dark, eerie places of rest.

The two walked past the last booth before the tent came.

"Step right up! Step right up and play this game and win the best prize of all!"

Gilbert saw that it was probably the most normal of the other games; which, of course, was very odd in this type of world. Yellow ducks floated in water traveling around in a circle. Gilbert had always loved those kinds of games because you always won something, whether it was a stuffed animal or a small plastic squirt gun. It was unlike the games for skilled people, throwing small plastic hoops over rows of bottles or trying to pop balloons that hung on a wall with darts—minus the splatter of blood inside.

"Step right up! Step right up!"

"Gilbert. Let's go," Wendell said, glancing back, noticing that Gilbert had stopped.

"Step right up, son! Won't you step right up and try this game out?"

Gilbert started to walk away.

"What, are you chicken, kid?" The voice clucked like a chicken.

What was weird was that none of the other loud speakers blared out those words or clucked. None of the others would really single you out and speak to you. It was like they were a recording playing over and over, unless you attempted to play the game and another voice changed its tone, explaining the rules.

"Hang on. I want to try this game," Gilbert said.

Wendell looked at the tent, then back at his friend. "I don't know, Gilbert. We need to go."

"I know we do. I want to save Rodney as soon as we can, but he isn't going anywhere, right?"

Wendell thought a minute. "Good point. Go ahead, if you must, but make it quick."

"Okay. One game. Then we'll go."

"Sounds fine."

As they approached the booth, the Ringmaster's voice echoed from the tent, beckoning the last members of the crowd who were entering inside: "Take a seat, my ghostly individuals! See my amazing show!"

"Welcome!" the same insulting voice blared out of the speaker. "Please choose a duck and read what is on it underneath. Fate awaits you! Everyone wins! A huge prize for every customer!"

Gilbert watched the ducks bob up and down, drifting aimlessly around and around inside the small channel of water. Each one was identical to the other. On the far wall hung chains, boots, and white sheets. Tools of the trade for being a ghost, he supposed.

Not wasting another minute, Gilbert snatched up a duck and looked at the bottom. A tiny blue screen scrolled across and said: WINNER! WINNER! WE ARE PROUD TO ANNOUNCE THAT YOU WILL HAVE A FRONT ROW SEAT BY ACCOMPANYING THE RINGMASTER IN THE CENTER OF THE SHOW! ALL EYES WILL BE ON YOU AS YOU ARE SURROUNDED BY THE CARNIVAL OF THE BIZARRE! LYCANTHROPES! ZOMBIES! AND THE *CANNIBALS!*

"Um. Wendell?"

"Find a good one, Gilbert?"

"Oh, I would say I did. You won't believe it. Here. Look at this."

Wendell's thick eyebrows rose, reading it.

"So, I get to be around the Ringmaster?"

"Right beside him. I'm not sure about this, Gilbert. This might be dangerous."

"I may be close enough to Rodney to free him. If he's brought out in front of the crowd."

"Oh, he'll be out there. I'm pretty sure of it. But you won't be able to do it alone. I think the best thing to do is to stay seated, watch the show until we get a chance to make our move. May have to wait until the place closes."

Gilbert wanted so much to be down in the center of the show. In the past, his parents had taken him to a carnival where the announcer selected someone out of the audience for a magic trick. He had never had the opportunity to do something like this. On the flipside, if Wendell said the Ringmaster was a bad dude, well, he believed him. Gilbert had second thoughts about being that close to the guy.

The Ringmaster's sidekick Tilbit had taken Rodney away only because of that mean old brother Gerald selling him. Gilbert also remembered that Wendell said he had a bone to pick with the Ringmaster. That was a mystery in itself. He wondered if it was related to the Tilbit incident long ago.

"Ready?" Wendell asked, pulling Gilbert out of his thoughts. "Let's go get a seat."

"Sure." Gilbert placed the duck back in the water, and as he walked away the voice out of the speaker barked: "Step right up! Step right up! Choose a duck! Choose your fate!"

* * * *

Inside the huge tent Wendell and Gilbert found a seat up high, in the very back. The way the place was set up, the stadium seats were arranged in a full circle, which gave the crowd a great view of the show below. Bright lights hung from above. Huge movie screens hung down for close-up shots of the show. And to retrieve any snacks, you never had to leave your seat. All you had to do was speak to a floating face of a clown on a small, bluish computer screen on the armrest of the seat. No charge for the snacks, either. However, the features of the clown—the bleached white face with dark circles painted around his slits for eyes, the blood-red nose, the pointy teeth revealed inside painted black lips every time he spoke a word, and the cone-shaped hat colored in black and silver—gave Gilbert a slight chill. He had never seen a clown made up like that. He figured that any ghost or werewolf or vampire or cannibal would not give the clown's features much thought. But since he was considered abnormal, he guessed he was supposed to look at certain things a bit differently.

"Hoo-hoo-hoo! I'm Poppy, your virtual server! Because I like to pop in and check on you from time to time," the clown said. "May I be of assistance?" He winked.

"Um. What kind of snacks do you have, Poppy?"

"Well," his snake-like tongue slipped out of his lips and

slid back in, "how about some popcorn to start? Freshest in the Sector!"

"Sure. Wendell, want some?"

"No. I'm fine."

"Comin' right up!" the clown said. "How 'bout a drink!"

Horrid thoughts of prune juice sifted through Gilbert's brain, souring his stomach. "What kind, uh, do you have?"

"Well, young man, we have water and prune juice and fruit juice and flavors of sparkling sodas."

Gilbert thought a minute. "What about the sodas? What kind of flavors do you have?"

"Strawberry, banana, cherry, lime and grape."

"I'll try lime, I guess."

"Hoo-hoo-hoo! Comin' right up!"

Two minutes later a bag of popcorn and a lime sparkling soda arrived on a floating tray held by a lone robotic hand. Gilbert took the popcorn and soda off of it and said thank you. The tray folded itself until it was a small rectangle and disappeared into a tiny slot inside the palm of the robot's hand; the hand gave a thumbs-up and drifted off.

Gilbert eyed the sparkling lime soda. Sniffed it. Took a drink. The flavor was tasty, and when he drank it reminded him of liquefied Pop Rocks that popped inside of your mouth. It was kinda cool!

"Wendell, if I'm served this stuff, what are the ghosts served?"

Wendell glanced around, trying to see if any spirits were snacking, found a few, but really couldn't make out what they were eating. It was strange to see a ghost do such a thing. "Gilbert, I really don't know. Good question though."

"Yeah, it's weird." He sat there a moment, then thought of an idea. To his surprise when he looked down, Poppy was staring back at him, a smile drawn under his red nose. Gilbert wondered how long Poppy had been there, staring, waiting for another order. "Poppy?" he asked.

"Hoo-hoo-hoo! Yes?"

"I've got a question."

"And I've got an answer."

"What kind of snacks do ghosts eat?"

"Why, there's ice-scream, Mr. Boo Bars, bags of spook-corn, Ghost-kisses, strands of licorice-flavored webs, spider-filled bags of—"

"Okay. I think I got the idea."

The lights suddenly went out, covering the place in total darkness. Poppy said goodbye and a lonely light appeared, shining directly upon the tall figure of the Ringmaster, who stood dead center under the tent.

"Welcome…welcome…*welcome* to the Carnival of the Bizarre, home of the impossible acts that could never be performed outside of this tent! My dear friends," his eyes sparkled in the light, "feast your eyes on THIS!" Everyone's gaze followed his finger where it pointed to a cage speared with a spotlight, holding a male zombie who was wearing bib overalls. The zombie wobbled and staggered.

Materializing out of the shadows came two silhouettes, two clowns who wore leather aprons and leather masks. In their hands they held hatchets. They opened the cage, stepped inside.

The air tensed and became cold, just like when Gilbert stepped through the female ghost back at the house he had been forbidden to enter. He wondered if it was because of all the ghosts-who sat, surrounding him and Wendell, possibly radiating fear like him. Then he thought: Why would a ghost be scared?

The leather-covered clowns wasted no time and attacked the zombie, hacking him up into bits and pieces. The crowd gasped. Flesh flew, blood splattered, the zombie's head fell from the shoulders and took a bounce off the ground and rolled against the inside of the cage. When the two ceased the slaughter they left the cage, dripping in the zombie's muck, escaping back into the shadows.

"What the heck was that all about? That's disgusting!" Gilbert whispered.

"Very much so," Wendell replied. "I'm not sure *what* it was all about."

"Now, watch CLOSELY!" the unseen voice of the Ring-master shouted.

Slowly, pieces of the zombie wiggled. The head rolled by itself across the ground. Severed hands and their fingers came together, reattaching themselves. The split-open chest and torso met, slapping together and making a wet, squishy sound. The legs and feet came together, followed by the head pressing onto the neck with another nasty sound. Soon the zombie came back together like a fleshy puzzle, stood, stared at the crowd and took a bow.

The crowd went wild. Wendell and Gilbert didn't find the act amusing and did not join in the response.

The light over the zombie went out, and the one over the Ringmaster came on. "Thank you! Thank you! Frank the Zombie thanks you!" When the crowd noise died down, he continued: "For our next act of the night, feast your ghostly eyes on THIS!" Again he pointed to a cage where a bright spotlight speared a werewolf inside.

The beast saw the crowd and immediately tried to break through the metal bars, causing the cage to rock. Drool drained from its mouth. The crowd gasped, pressed against their ghostly backs against their seats. The beast's green eyes stared at the crowd. There was a loud *pop!* and from behind the creature came a large mechanical claw that reached out and grabbed and pulled the werewolf into the middle of the cage. Struggling, the lycanthrope was bound in its grip.

Gilbert felt Wendell move in his seat. He could tell he did not like what he saw. Wendell's hands squeezed the armrests.

A figure of a clown emerged out of the shadows carrying a rifle, entered the cage, turned to the crowd, held up a silver bullet, smiled, loaded it, turned, took aim and fired right into the skull of the werewolf. Quick. Sudden death.

The werewolf collapsed.

The crowd did not make a noise.

The armrest under Wendell's seat gripped and began to crack.

The clown exited out of the cage, slipped into the darkness.

Seconds rolled by as the mechanical claw let go, allowing the werewolf's body to drop with a thump and sprawl out on the ground, bleeding from its wound. From the complete silence under the tent, a splinter of a man's bone could be heard if dropped.

Then the unbelievable happened. The werewolf twitched and began rising, finally standing upright. With two long fingernails it dug into the bone and flesh under the fur of its skull and pulled free the silver bullet. Gilbert saw the beast's huge mouth filled with razor-sharp teeth pull back into a smile as it took a bow.

The crowd cheered. Went wild. Gilbert only sat there, not speaking. He thought the trick was neat, like the zombie's, but did not want to say it was or clap or cheer because of Wendell sitting beside him, seething about the situation. That would be rude.

The spotlight went out over the werewolf and reappeared over the Ringmaster. "How about that, folks!" He threw his hands up in the air, and the crowd cheered and whistled. When the noise died away, he said, "Our next part of the show is amazing. Be prepared, folks, be *prepared*!"

The light deadened over the Ringmaster and came alive over a cage where an old wooden coffin sat. Slowly, it creaked open by itself. A hand with long, boney fingernails gripped the side. A pale bald head emerged; two red eyes sunken back in their sockets peeked at the crowd, as the vampire climbed out and stood with a black cape drawn around him. His pale flesh drew taut against his face. Razor-sharp fangs were revealed behind curled lips. He stared intently at the crowd, scanning their ghostly forms.

Entering out of the shadows was a clown dressed in a cloak, holding a huge cross and a mallet hung on one hip; on the other hip hung a wooden stake.

Gilbert sat on the edge of his seat.

Immediately, the vampire felt the clown's presence as it stepped into the cage. The vampire hissed. His red eyes grew wide. The cross was pressed against the air, showing the Lord's force against the vampire as the creature drew backward, holding an open claw in front of its face, continuing its hissing. Within minutes the clown forced the vampire to return to his coffin, dropped the cross, and pulled free the wooden stake and mallet.

The clown took a second to turn sideways toward the audience, smiled, and proceeded to do his work as the stake disappeared inside the coffin and the mallet rose, fell, following with the wet smack into flesh and a shriek that crawled across the flesh of Gilbert's back. Both of the vampire's hands shot out, clawing the air, trembling in pain. An arc of blood shot up. Another splattered the clown and dripped down onto the floor.

The pounding of the stake echoed under the tent until the shrieking ceased and the man was soaked with vampire blood. He wiped his forehead, exited the cage.

Minutes went by, and no one in the audience made a sound.

Suddenly a hand shot up out of the coffin, the long boney

fingers wide open, then disappeared and came back with the stake saturated with blood in its boney grip. The stake was tossed to the side where it made wet, red spots across the cage's floor. The vampire rose, and his chest blossomed red. He climbed out and held up his hands and took a bow.

The crowd went wild.

"How are they doing all of this, Wendell?" Gilbert asked.

"I don't know. I think there's some kind of black magic involved here."

"Black magic? Like witchcraft?"

"I wouldn't doubt the Ringmaster's morbid sense of humor, but I didn't think it could be true."

The light shut off over the caged vampire and flicked on over the Ringmaster. "How about that, my ghostly crowd? Mmmm?"

The crowd went wild again, clapping.

"Now." The applause died to a murmur. "Our next part of the show is not for the squeamish; not for the light at heart. No. Not at all! Be prepared for what you will see, my friends! Remember when I told you there was something that will make your corpses roll in their graves? Mmmm? Here it is! Watch, as our cannibal feasts on a victim right before your hollow eyes! Watch *closely*!" The Ringmaster's finger shot to the left, and the light speared another cage where Rodney stood all alone, a scared look flashing across his features.

"The Ringmaster has Rodney down there!" Gilbert snapped and pointed. "Look at him! He's scared to death!"

"I see him, Gilbert," Wendell replied.

Surfacing out of the shadows were two clowns pulling Bobby in shackles and chains. They opened the cage's door and pushed him inside, where he stumbled and fell.

Gilbert's stomach felt like a cold, dark pit. Horror washed over him, draining the happiness from his skin. He was at a loss for words. These terrible people had both of his friends together, forcing Rodney to do what he did best: eat human flesh!

"We need to do something!"

"We need to wait, Gilbert. I'm not so sure that we can save Rodney right away."

Wendell did not understand the situation at hand. He did not realize that down in the cage stood his best buddy with Rodney. "That's Bobby down there with Rodney, Wendell!" Gilbert snapped. "We need to save them! I think they're gonna force Rodney to eat Bobby!"

Wendell glanced at him, down at the cage, then back. Now it registered. "Damn it! Okay. Hang on, let me think about this!"

One of the clowns stepped into the cage, grabbed Bobby's arm, pulled out a blade and sliced open a gash on top of his forearm. Bobby cried out from the sting. His blood started oozing from the wound, coloring the ground red.

The clown left, shutting the cage's door.

"Those bastards!" Gilbert spat. "We need to do something, Wendell!"

* * * *

Rodney was frightened to death. But with a familiar smell in the air, a copper aroma, he licked his lips, glaring at the boy who bled. A hunger started surging inside of his stomach. This kid had not been mean to him. He had not called him names. He wasn't a threat to Rodney.

But it was the flavor of blood that he desired! A taunting, as if invisible crimson fingers led him forward. It had been a long time since he'd had a taste. A nip.

Maybe that was all he needed to get over the ravaging hunger inside, a small, succulent taste…

* * * *

"This is what we'll do, Gilbert," Wendell finally said. "I'm going to cause a diversion. When I do, go get your friends."

"What are you gonna do?"

"You'll see. Get ready."

* * * *

The hunger for flesh and blood coursed through Rodney's veins. His eyes found Bobby and he knew his victim was scared. He could smell it. The victim held his arm, trying to stop the bleeding by squeezing it, which did not do much good…

Wendell left his chair in a fury and raced down to where the action was going on. He slammed the cage, rocking it, while inside, Bobby turned his head, shocked. Rodney did not, drawn in like a tractor beam.

Wendell grabbed the bars and shook them, yelling something that Gilbert could not make out, and started to howl.

Slipping out of the shadows, three clowns grabbed Wendell, trying to pull him away. He didn't let go—instead he held tight. Another clown came to help, finally making

Wendell lose his grip, and the four dragged him backward until he stumbled, then they stumbled, collapsing like a pyramid of cards.

A light came on over the Ringmaster, and he shouted, "Get him out of here! Kick that fool out of the door and shut it!"

Gilbert watched as Wendell broke free. He was tackled by two more clowns and slammed the ground. Now there were a total of six clowns fighting to get him out of the tent and away from the show.

Gilbert left his seat and raced down to the cage as fast as he could.

* * * *

A little taste of blood, Rodney thought. *A smidgen of a taste and old Rodney would be fine. Yes, yes.* He felt the drooling hunger growling inside of his stomach. He saw the victim's eyes widen in horror...

"*Rodney!*" a familiar voice spoke, but the hunger overrode it.

Rodney hadn't had raw, human flesh in quite awhile...

"*Rodney!*"

That's right, victim, breakfastlunchandsupper, draw back against the cage. Don't fight it. Don't fight it. It will only be worse if you do...hey?

Someone was grabbing his arm.

It was his friend, Gilbert. *Gilbert?*

"Gilbert?" Rodney shook his head. "Wha-What's going on?" He rubbed his face and eyes. He blinked. He looked over at the victim pressing himself against the cage.

"You can't eat him, Rodney! That's my best friend!" Gilbert snapped, pointing to the terrified boy.

A pause followed as Rodney let it all sink in and swish around. "I thought *I* was your best friend, Gilbert?"

"You are my friend."

"Not your best friend? I thought you liked me?"

Gilbert shook his head, knew he didn't have time for Rodney's quirky remarks and confusing sentences. "Look. We need to get out of here. Wendell over there has his hands full and diverted attention so I can break you two out! Luckily they didn't lock the cage door. If they had, you might have eaten Bobby."

"Oh! Now! I told you before I only eat bad people."

"You were about to eat Bobby! He's not bad!"

"But... He's bleeding. All I wanted was a small nip."

"Nip?"

"Yeah, sip."

"You said nip!"

Rodney blinked. "No I didn't. I said sip."

"Rodney!" Gilbert threw his hands up. "Look. Let's make like a tree and split."

"Do what?"

"Nothing." Gilbert did not have time to explain and glanced over at Wendell. He was losing the battle, and they were dragging him away. He looked at Bobby. "You okay?"

"Yep." The fear left his expression and happiness arrived. "'Bout time you showed up! I almost got eaten by this freak here!"

"Bobby! He's not a freak! He's a friend of mine!"

"He almost ate me!"

Rodney stood there sulking, head down.

"It's a disease. He can't help it! I stopped him from attacking you, that's the important thing! End of story!"

"I know, but—"

"No buts! Done! Over with! We need to get outta here!"

"I've been with this carnival for a few days. It's been crazy!"

"You'll never guess where *I've* been. It's been crazier! I'll tell you all about it later, okay? Right now we need to get you out of those shackles and chains."

"Okay."

Gilbert looked around to see if maybe there was a rung of keys lying on the ground, by chance. There wasn't. "We'll just have to figure out how to get you out of those later. C'mon!"

Gilbert helped Bobby along and left the cage, with Rodney following close behind. All this time, the crowd had been silent. Gilbert saw that each ghost sat there gazing. He wondered if they thought this was all part of the show.

The opening to the tent that led outside was close, only a few feet away. Gilbert did not see Wendell anywhere inside.

"And where do you three think you are going?" the Ringmaster's voice boomed as he slithered out of the dark, stepping in front of them. "Think that you can come in here and wreck my show? Mmmm? Think that you can throw a wrench in the machine? Mmmm?"

"Get out of our way! We are leaving!" Gilbert spat.

"Not. Until," he pointed, "I. Have. My SHOW!" He lunged and snatched Bobby, pulling him beside him. "He's mine! I'm gonna bleed 'im!"

Rodney's face twisted. "Give our friend back! Now!"

"And what are *you* gonna do about it? Huh? Freak? Retard? Who ever heard of a kid who eats human flesh! It isn't normal!"

Behind Rodney's eyes a flame grew, scorching him from the inside. Anger blossomed and, without warning, he attacked the Ringmaster, pushing him down on the ground. Taking one huge hand, he pulled his face off, showing the workings of the machine underneath.

"Go! Get Bobby out of here, Gilbert! I'll be along in a second!"

Shocked at what had just arisen, Gilbert grabbed Bobby, who had stumbled to the side and exited the tent. Immediately, they saw Wendell, now in full werewolf form. He was fighting the clowns, throwing them this way and that. Since they were robots, too, they would only slam the ground, hardly harmed, rise and run forward after the lycanthrope.

Wendell's green eyes saw Gilbert and Bobby.

A single clown rushed Wendell. With one swipe his hairy claw decapitated the clown. Sparks shot out of the stump, and the body collapsed and convulsed. Two more clowns returned their attack only to find that their end repeated the last clown's. Each of their heads took a roll across the ground. The painted eyes and lips twitched.

Wendell attacked three more clowns and ripped their bodies in half. Sparks flew. Bodies convulsed.

Gilbert gasped at the scene. He'd had no idea that Wendell was that strong. No wonder the Baron was scared of him and his kind.

"Where's Rodney?" Wendell growled and stepped over in front of Gilbert. Bobby cringed and stepped backward, gazing up at the beast.

Gilbert said, "No need to worry about Wendell, Bobby. He's on our side. A friend of mine. Right?"

Wendell smiled, showing off his razor-sharp teeth.

Bobby cringed again.

"Rodney's back there taking care of the Ringmaster," Gilbert explained.

"Really?" Wendell asked. "Does he need help?"

"Nope. He, uh, tore the guy's face off."

"And it was mighty tasty," Rodney said, coming up behind them, licking his fingers.

Gilbert turned. "You *ate* him?"

"Some of him."

"He's a robot!"

"Sorta."

"Sorta?"

"Yeah. Sorta. He's sorta flesh and sorta blood over his shell. It was artificial, but very similar in taste. Pretty good!"

Gilbert's stomach soured a bit. "If you say so, Rodney."

"We need to get through the door and get as far away as we can," Wendell informed them. "I saw Tilbit running off, probably snitching to the Baron what happened. He'll be on our tails in a hurry."

"I would love to find a way out of this world and back to my own," Gilbert said.

"Same here," Bobby added. "Um. What about these chains?"

"Oh, sorry. I can take care of that," Wendell said and snapped them apart with his claws as if they were made of plastic.

"Thanks." Bobby smiled and rubbed his wrists.

"No problem. Follow me, guys. We're hittin' the ro—"

"Not so fast, lycanthrope!" a voice snaked out of the air.

When Gilbert and his group turned, there stood the vampire, the zombie, and the werewolf.

Wendell growled. "What do you want?" Bobby, Gilbert, and Rodney stood behind the hairy beast.

The vampire said nothing. He stepped forward, and in a blink of an eye he stood face to face with Wendell.

The vampire curled his lips, the rack of jagged fangs showing. "We would," he hissed, "like to thank you for free-ing us."

The zombie and the werewolf followed suit.

"We have been prisoners here with the Ringmaster for quite awhile. There are more of us, trapped behind bars, who will be freed. We are forever in your debt, lycanthrope."

"It's Wendell," he said and shook hands with the vampire. "You do not need to repay us. Thank you."

"As you wish, Wendell. I am Vlad, and my esteemed colleagues are Nevil"—the zombie raised a hand to wave—"and Thomas." The werewolf nodded.

Wendell nodded back, introduced Bobby, Gilbert, and Rodney.

"How did the Ringmaster pull those tricks off?" Gilbert asked.

The vampire's red eyes lowered, peering down at Gilbert. "Tricks?"

"Yeah. When they drove a stake through your heart. When they chopped up Ned. When they shot Adam. You all still lived. How'd he do that?"

The vampire grinned. "Voodoo. The Ringmaster somehow found a way to practice voodoo. The silver bullet for Adam, there," he pointed to the werewolf, "was very real but obviously didn't kill him."

"Hurt like hell!" Adam snarled.

"Yes. So it did." Vlad eyed Adam. "The stake didn't really puncture my heart because I've never owned one to begin with. The vampire who attacked me—dreadful fellow—bit my neck, and he didn't stop there. No. It all ended up getting a bit messy because he tore my heart out and ate it."

"That's disgusting!" Bobby said.

"Quite so, lad. You can say that I'm the poster child for the living dead."

"What about the zombie?" Gilbert asked.

"Ned? That's a natural thing for him. Odd...but natural. With or without voodoo he can repair himself. Unless he's set on fire."

"That's weird."

"Very much so. Bizarre."

"Well," Wendell said, "we need to go. Good luck."

"And good luck to you, Wendell," the vampire said, bowing.

The three members of the Carnival of the Bizarre watched as Wendell and Gilbert walked through the doorway, Bobby and Rodney in tow.

* * * *

They stepped through the carnival's doorway and, after taking a few steps, suddenly realized something was wrong. The scenery had changed. Briar had disappeared. The old buildings had vanished and left a desolate, flat land full of graves and gravestones.

"Um. Wendell?" Gilbert asked. "Where are we?"

"I think we just stepped into another Sector," Wendell responded with a growl, scratching his hairy ear. "The one I've heard about before."

"How could that be? We stepped back through the same door we entered through."

"Don't know. I've heard there are such things as doors that are the wrong ones to go through."

"They're apparitions," Rodney added.

"Say what?" Gilbert asked. "A ghost door?"

"Yep. They exist. Saw them before."

Gilbert chuckled. "What the heck would a ghost door do? Surely it couldn't be a threat. How could we just walk into another Sector?"

"Yes we could. They trick you, posing as the door you just stepped through. Like now. If they were murdered somewhere—"

"You mean like destroyed?"

"Yep. They would return as ghosts."

"So, you think that was a ghost door we just now walked through?"

"Yep."

Gilbert turned to look at the door. It was gone. "Hey! What the heck happened to the other one?"

While the others took notice, too, Rodney explained very nonchalantly: "Oh, it might have gotten tired of hanging around and took off. Usually their hinges start whining if the ghost doors have to stay in one spot very long."

"Took. Off?" Gilbert asked. "Rodney, doors don't just take off." He looked at Wendell for help.

He shrugged his hairy shoulders.

"Sure they do. Think you're the only one who walks through them? They know others need a threshold to walk over, and they like tricking others too. Sounds to me like you may be a little selfish." Rodney puckered his lips, folded his arms across his chest.

"What? Me? Selfish? Rodney, you just told me that they trick people. Why would someone else be waiting to step through them?"

"Because they don't know they'll be tricked. Like this door just did to us. And, I think you're a bit selfish about it, too."

"How can I be selfish about it?"

"You just are."

Gilbert shook his head, decided not to continue this conversation. "This is way too much for me to swallow!" He threw his hands up in the air for the second time tonight.

"Swallow?" Rodney's head tipped to the side. "Swallow what? The door?"

"Ahhhggggg! No! No! It's hard for me to understand all of this." Gilbert closed his eyes, placed both hands on each side of his head. "Ooooh…I think I'm gettin' a headache!" His hands slid forward, covering his face.

As if a light bulb had winked on over Rodney's head, he said: "Ah. I see what you're-saying now."

Bobby came up beside Gilbert. "Is this world really *this* confusing?"

"Yes." Gilbert's reply was a muffled response through his fingers. "Especially as told by Rodney."

"And there are some doors that are even two-way doors," Rodney began, "like two-way mirrors, where from one side you can see through, but from the other you cannot—"

"Save it, Rodney! Please," Gilbert warned. "I'm trying to *not* be so confused."

"Save what?"

Gilbert sighed. "Save your story for later."

"Oh. Sure, Gilbert."

"Boys? We need to move," Wendell said, now standing off to the side. "I can't see any farther than all the graves. I'm not sure what else there is." He stood there as darkness pressed in from each side and the only light they had to see by was the full moon above.

The group agreed with Wendell, following behind the hairy beast.

"Hey, can't you change back to human form?" Bobby asked.

"Well, I'd like to. Problem is, I don't have any clothes to wear. Sorta, uh, ripped them apart back there, fighting those clowns."

"Oh." Bobby looked up at the moon. "Good thing that's shining, huh?"

"Yep," Wendell said, gazing up at it himself, noticing the haze around it. Stars twinkled, painted over the dark canvas of the sky. "If it wasn't full I might be running around here naked." He smiled.

Bobby returned the gesture with a chuckle and said, "It's really weird talking to a werewolf."

"Why is that?"

"Back in my and Gilbert's world they don't exist."

"I think Gilbert mentioned that. You two must have an odd world."

"Not really. It's got its bad points at times."

"Like what?"

"We have to go to school and have to eat our Brussels sprouts."

"Sounds odd."

"It's more than that. It's torture! Ever tried to eat Brussels sprouts?"

"Can't say that I have."

"Good thing, then. They're nasty tastin'."

The gang noticed gravestones standing erect out of the

157

soil, some even leaning to the side like the Leaning Tower of Pisa. Each stone was blank, minus an inscription for the dead buried below, which Gilbert found weird. Why would someone not write something about the dead? Something respectful, such as "Here Lies…whomever."

"Bobby, what happened to you when you went through that door in the old house? Where'd you disappear to?"

"Disappear? I never left the house."

"You weren't there when I went looking for you."

"That's funny. I went looking for you, too, right after I saw a shadow slip out of the window in the room. Remember what we saw in the hallway? Those shadows peeking out of the rooms?"

Gilbert rummaged through his memory bank. "Yeah. I remember them."

"I saw that shadow, like I said, then walked back out into the hallway and you were gone."

"I was there! I went looking for you!"

"Really? That's weird. I searched the entire floor and didn't see you."

"That house was bad news!" Gilbert sighed. "Shoulda listened to my parents."

"Guess they were right about telling us to stay away from it."

"Yep."

Gilbert tipped his head to the side. "But how did you end up at the Carnival?"

"When I went to the next floor and walked into a room I ended up in a castle."

"Castle?"

"Yep. I ended up in this huge castle."

"No kiddin'?"

"Nope."

"So, anyway, I started walking down the corridor and was chased by these weird creatures with glowing yellow eyes wearing dark hooded cloaks."

"Did you just say figures in hooded cloaks with yellow eyes?" Wendell said over his shoulder.

"Yep. I couldn't see their faces."

"Creepy," Wendell concluded.

"And they chased me for I don't know how long until I finally got away from them by climbing up a ladder that sat smack-dab in the middle another corridor."

"Did it go anywhere? Like up on a balcony or roof?" Gilbert asked.

"No. Nothing like that." Bobby chuckled, rubbed a hand through his hair. "It went into a hole in the air. An actual hole in the air! It was wild! I ended up in this long tunnel that seemed like a ventilation system."

Gilbert was at a loss for words.

"But when I finally found a way out I was snatched up by Tilbit. I had been wandering down a dirt road, and when Tilbit rode by on his horse and carriage, he offered me a ride, told me he could help me, and then threw some handcuffs on my wrists."

"That's terrible!" Rodney said. "That dude threw cuffs on me too when he delivered me to the carnival!"

"Tilbit has a history of being a really bad guy, you three,"

Wendell explained. "He's been around for quite a while and has worked for the Ringmaster for years."

"Not anymore he doesn't. Thanks to Rodney," Gilbert said with a grin, laying a hand on Rodney's shoulder. The cannibal smiled back at him.

"That's right, Gilbert," Wendell agreed. "Rodney took care of that morbid show that should have never been started—and its leader too."

"So, Gilbert, how did you end up in this world?" Bobby asked.

"Man, it is a long story." Gilbert sighed. "Where shall I begin? Let's see. After I came out of the room, I—"

"Shhh!" Wendell had stopped, his ears perked up, and he sniffed the air.

"What's wrong?" Gilbert asked.

For a second or two Wendell stood there frozen, not speaking. Then: "I thought I heard something."

"What did you hear?" Bobby asked.

"Scratching."

Gilbert looked behind him, noticing all the graves that spread out, pushing out into the darkness. To him, the place was eerie. "Wendell, what kind of scratching did you hear?"

"It sounded like something scratching on wood."

"Huh."

"Let's keep going," Wendell said.

The group hadn't moved ten feet when Wendell halted again. This time he held his hairy right arm and hand out as if to protect them. "Something isn't right here. I sense something evil."

"Um. Did you just say 'evil'?" Gilbert asked.

"Yes."

A small breeze blew. The moon's radiance highlighted the gravestones, turning them a ghostly white.

"What do you think it is?" Bobby asked.

"I don't know. It may be——"

"Look!" Rodney shouted, pointing to a grave nearby. They all watched as the soil sunk inward and a decrepit hand shot out, gripping the air with its decayed fingers. Another beside it emerged, followed with a growing head and shoulders. Dead flesh hung from the jaws of the zombie's face. One of its hollow eyes spilled maggots, and something slithered out between the rotten teeth as if the corpse had caught it in his throat and coughed it up. When the thing hit the dirt it scurried away.

The corpse pulled itself free, stood, reached out with a twisted hand, the fingers all broken except the pinky, and pointed at the traveling bunch who stood there, appalled by the sight of the living dead. Its head was thrown back, and it managed a garble of words that none of them could understand.

"Um. Time to go." Gilbert was surprised he could say it with his throat feeling as if it was trying to lock up, trying to create a wall so the words couldn't pass through. But, obviously, they must have paid the toll and were delivered promptly.

"You hit the nail on the head that time, buddy," Bobby said.

Rodney frowned. "Hit the what on the *what?*"

"Explain later," Gilbert said quickly. "Time to go!"

"Stay close. Follow me!" Wendell growled.

The quartet took off, and around them the dirt on top of the other graves fell inward, sinking like quicksand, drawing out their inhabitants one by one. The aroma of the dead filled the air as the population buried underground rose.

Gilbert stayed close behind Wendell while Bobby and Rodney trailed behind, swerving to miss each corpse who tried to reach out for them. A crusty hand brushed Rodney's face, and he yelped.

For some odd reason, Gilbert was reminded of the time he visited a make-believe haunted house on Halloween and had to walk through a very slender hallway while hands on both sides tried to grab him through prison bars.

Gilbert snuck a glance over his shoulder at Rodney and asked, "Hungry?"

"Heck no! I'm not eatin' any of *that!*"

Bobby smiled.

A crowd of the dead stepped in front of the travelers, and Wendell suddenly became a quarterback, knocking bodies out of the way as he ran. Pieces of them tore apart and littered the ground. A hand plopped down on top of Gilbert's head and bounced off, startling him.

"Look!" Bobby shouted. "There's a doorway!"

And, sure enough, there was. It sat to their right, tipped to the side, the bottom edge sunk into the ground. Wendell ran for it, growling at the others to follow.

Rodney stumbled over a tombstone, fell, and accidently

hit Bobby's leg with his huge hand, causing them both to slam hard against the ground.

Gilbert ran four more feet before noticing the two. "Hold on, Wendell! We need to save Bobby and Rodney!"

The werewolf looked back, saw them, and said, "Get to the door! I'll save 'em!"

Gilbert ran. Before he reached the door a hand shot out of the ground, grabbing his ankle, and he went sprawling to the dirt. Two more hands pushed out and held him down, keeping him from trying to rise back up. He tried to shout for Wendell, but another hand that smelled so bad he almost hurled through its dead fingers shot out of the ground and covered his mouth.

Wendell ran back and started helping both boys up. Another hand reached out of the ground and grabbed his hairy leg. When he tried to pull free, a corpse came with it. The legs had rotted off and only the torso, arms, and a head with a missing lower jaw and black beetles spilling out of both eyes remained intact.

With one swipe of Wendell's claw, the corpse's head left its shoulders and rolled across three graves where more of the dead were slowly rising up. But the grip held. The headless, dead chunk of the body hung taut onto the hairy leg.

Using his other foot Wendell stamped the arm, smashing it flat, severing it away from the elbow—and it still held! "Run to the door! Gilbert should be th—" Wendell shouted and saw Gilbert being held flat on the ground.

Ten feet from him staggered a large crowd of the dead.

This was an ambush of zombies.

"Get to the door, Bobby and Rodney! Hurry!" Wendell barked at them as he reached down, pulled the severed limb off and threw it at an incoming zombie so it hit him square in the face. The limb grabbed the throat and squeezed, not even making the corpse change direction, or stop moving, as the limb dangled, hanging on like an extra passenger on a ride.

Bobby and Rodney had only made it five feet before hands shot out of the ground and grabbed their ankles, causing them to suffer an exact repeat of what had happened to Gilbert. When the two hit the ground, they began to sink as if the soil had mysteriously turned to quicksand. And within seconds they were gone from the surface.

Wendell saw it happen. Before he could save Gilbert, the ground opened up like a huge mouth and swallowed him whole, leaving his muffled cry for help behind.

Zombies surrounded Wendell. He began fighting them as the ground beneath him gave way and he too, like the others, sunk into the soil as if they had all been buried alive.

* * * *

Voices brought Gilbert out of his slumber in an underground stone crypt. Dome lights hung overhead, shining down. Metal cuffs wrapped his wrists, chaining them to the stone wall. He was slumped, his legs bent at the knee. He straightened up. As he focused his eyes on the blond mop hanging off the large scalp beside him, excitement ran through his veins. "Rodney! You okay?"

Rodney turned his head and when he saw Gilbert, he

smiled. "Hey, Gilbert! I was wondering when you were going to wake up."

Gilbert's eyes soaked in the horrid sights of the room. Chains with metal cuffs hung on each of the four walls. In the corner lay a skeleton, held in chains, clean of flesh. An archway into darkness lay to his right.

"Where's Bobby and Wendell?"

"Don't know. All I remember is waking up here in chains."

Gilbert could only remember sinking into the ground and the soil bleeding into his mouth and his nose, feeling as if it would all drain down into his stomach, fill up his lungs, cutting off his very last breath. While that feeling *was* there, it didn't happen, as if it was something to trick his mind into thinking it would. "We need to find a way out of here and not end up like *that* guy." Gilbert nodded his head toward the skeleton.

"Yeah," he agreed, "don't want to end up like that."

Rodney felt an itch and slid his wrist out of the metal cuff and scratched his nose. Satisfied, he wiggled his fingers and wrist back through.

Gilbert didn't notice this, instead looking at the archway. "Wonder where that leads?"

"Looks spooky," Rodney said. "I've been staring at it, thinking I'd see a zombie walk through."

Gilbert pulled on the chains, leaning forward as hard as he could, but they wouldn't detach from the wall. He tried to pull his wrists free from the cuffs without any luck. His face was flushed with frustration. "Maybe we'll get lucky and Wendell will break out of any hold they've got him in."

Rodney's uncontrollable itch returned, and he slid his wrist back out and scratched his nose. "Do you really think he could break free?"

"He should be able to. He's a were—" Gilbert turned his head just in time to notice Rodney fumbling to slip his wrist back through the cuff while finishing his sentence, "wolf."

He stared at Rodney.

"What's wrong, Gilbert?" Rodney said.

Gilbert frowned.

"What's wrong? You okay?"

"I'm fine." His voice was sharp. "How is it that your hand was out of the cuff?"

For a second Rodney didn't speak, trying to put the right words together. "I had an itch that needed to be scratched."

"You mean to tell me you can get out of your chains?" Gilbert inquired.

"No. I said I had an itch that needed to be scratched."

"Rodney. I just saw you slipping your wrist back in the chains. You got your hand out of it, right?"

"Yep."

"So you can get out of your chains."

"Yep."

"You watched me tug and pull on these things," he rattled the chains, "and you already knew how to get out of them?"

"Yep."

"Geez! I can't believe this! Why didn't you just slip out

of yours and help me?"

"Because I didn't think we were supposed to. We're imprisoned. We're not supposed to get out. You've said so yourself."

Gilbert did remember the discussion earlier when he'd tried to explain to Rodney that if you are in prison, you stay in prison. You don't wander around outside of it taking a stroll. So, defeated, Gilbert replied: "Okay. You're right. I said that. But this is different! We need to get out of this and try and find Wendell and Bobby—who knows where he is!—and get the heck outta here!"

"Okay. Hang on." Rodney slipped one wrist out of the metal cuff, then the other. He stepped in front of Gilbert. "Can you get your wrist out?"

Gilbert shook his head, disgusted. "No, you saw me try! I can't get my wrist out like you. Don't you think I'd be free by now if I could?"

Rodney held a blank expression for about half a minute before he replied, "Oh. Yeah. Guess you're right."

"Is there any way you can help me? Can you possibly bend metal?"

"Not that I know of. I'll try." Rodney started pulling on the chain, trying to pull it out of the wall. When that didn't work, he tried to pull one of Gilbert's cuffs apart. That didn't work either.

Gilbert sighed, a bit more disgusted now. "I don't know what we are going to do."

"You will come with me," a voice said, making both boys

nearly jump out of their skin. When Gilbert and Rodney looked, a zombie stood in the doorway. One of its eyes was missing, and a long worm slid out of one of its nostrils and fell to the floor, wiggling. It made Gilbert think of a green glob of snot.

Decrepit hands reached out and released Gilbert's chains with a key. A putrid aroma hung thick in the air, and Gilbert fought back the urge to puke.

A few more worms fell out of the zombie's nose, hitting Gilbert's sneakers and bouncing off of them.

Gilbert's stomach flip-flopped.

* * * *

Minutes later Gilbert and Rodney exited through the archway, following the dead guy down a corridor at a slow pace. At first, the hallway had been flooded with darkness, until dome lights blazed overhead. Every time the group would pass under them, they would shut off in their wake as if they worked on a motion sensor.

Gilbert's mind twisted and turned, thinking he would see something lurking in the dark as soon as the lights overhead came on. But there was nothing. He had no idea where his other two friends were. He hoped that they were still alive, that they hadn't been slaughtered. Judging from the scary movies he had seen, zombies usually did that sort of thing. They usually liked to eat people.

Usually.

But he did remember that he was in another kind of world where you could befriend a cannibal and a werewolf, and watch a Carnival of the Bizarre led by an insane robot covered in artificial flesh in a town populated with ghosts.

Gilbert sighed. He felt drained of energy, both mentally and physically. If he mentioned something like that around his father, he would always be reminded of how easy he had it with: "Tired? Gilbert, when I was your age I rose at the crack of dawn, milked the cows, fed the chickens, plowed the field with your grandfather, and fit breakfast in around eight a.m. You're too young to be tired. You should have lots and lots of energy."

Truth was, Gilbert really didn't feel that he had much.

Easier said than done, Dad, he thought and shook his head.

So, the trio walked farther, and more lights flicked on and off overhead. Eventually they came to steps that led down into more darkness. He only hoped that lights would flick on at the bottom step.

When they did, he wasn't so sure that the scenery would not have been better left in darkness. Then again, maybe not: old wooden coffins stood upright, lining the walls in a huge room.

"Wonder why all of these coffins are in here instead of buried?" Gilbert asked aloud.

"Don't know," Rodney said without turning around.

They passed all the coffins and went through a door and down another flight of stairs. Before the door shut by itself, the dome lights went out in the room. At the end of the steps, another long corridor unfolded before the three, and yet another door stood waiting for their entrance. In the walls there was scratching and something scurrying, making the hairs on the back of the two boys' necks stand erect.

At the end of the hall the zombie opened the door, stood to the side, and said: "Enter. Zebulla is waiting."

Gilbert stepped inside after Rodney and saw a figure dressed in a long black dress seated at the front of the room. The color infusing her face was ash-gray. Veins pushed against the surface of her cheeks as if they were canals running in her dead flesh. Her hair lay on her bony shoulders. Her cracked lips pulled back into a smile under her nose, and she said, "Welcome. Please," she motioned with a hand to a row of church pews off to the side, "have a seat."

Two zombies stood on each side of her holding swords.

Gilbert and Rodney each took a seat, and the pew moaned from their weight.

The woman licked her lips, allowing her eyes to fall on one of the boys. A bug slipped from her mouth and scurried across the floor. She said, "I presume that your name is Gilbert. Correct?"

"Uh. Yeah."

One of her eyes rolled to Rodney, while the other stayed fixated on Gilbert. "And you, child, are Rodney. Correct?"

"Y-Yeah," Rodney replied.

She chuckled. "You two looked scared out of your skin. Boys, there is nothing to be afraid of here. Everything is sorted out. You are not our enemy. Wendell has informed us of your recent travels."

At ease now, Gilbert asked, "Is Bobby okay?"

"Yes. The rest of your party will return very soon."

"What are they doing?"

The woman coughed, held her hand over her mouth, but didn't block out the maggots that fell into her lap. "Excuse me." She wiped her lap clean. "They were held in chains," she continued, "like you two, but in a different part of the underground."

"Oh," Gilbert replied and just so happened to look up to see that the ceiling was marred with numerous cracks.

The woman noticed his gaze and explained, "The ceiling is beyond repair. The weight of the surface pushes down so much that it takes a lot of work keeping the structure of the ceiling intact."

"Ma'am," Gilbert said.

"Please. Call me Zebulla."

"Zebulla. Why were we in chains?"

"We wanted to make sure you were not a threat to us. Like I have just said, everything has been explained. I have been told that you hold a grudge against the Baron as we do. He is a very mean individual. One of these days he will be stopped and made to pay for his violent actions."

"So, where are we exactly?"

"You are in the Land of the Dead. We were all once human beings that roamed Hearth." She paused. "Until the Baron took our flesh and blood away, turning them into machines, placing our souls in these decayed bodies to rot away."

"Don't you go to Heaven when you die, or something?"

Zebulla's face clouded, making Gilbert sit back, as her

voice boomed, "Heaven has shut its doors on the planet of Hearth. No one leaves."

A cold punch in the gut hit Gilbert.

"It is because of the Baron and his horrible, filthy acts of punishments!" Zebulla said. "He started the book on converting all adults into robots long ago."

"I have read some of the Book of Bloth," Gilbert said. "It seems terrible to do such a thing to an adult."

"It is very terrible to do it to a human being."

Gilbert thought a minute, said, "So, all of your bodies hold the souls that the Baron killed?"

"Yes, Gilbert."

"What happened to the souls who were the original owners of the bodies?"

"We don't know. We only hope they left this dreadful life for the next."

"And what about the ghosts in the ghost town we went through?"

"Ghost town, you ask?" Zebulla's head tipped to the side.

"Yes," Wendell said as he and Bobby stepped into the room, escorted by a zombie. Gilbert and Rodney's faces brightened at their arrival. The werewolf had turned back into a man and he had found some clothes, borrowed from a coffin. "It was where I told you the Ringmaster and Tilbit held their Carnival of the Bizarre." Wendell's eyes fell on Gilbert and Rodney. "Hey, guys? How are you two?"

"Just fine," Gilbert replied.

"Yep," Rodney added.

"I remember now, Wendell. I apologize. Sometimes my memory isn't what it used to be."

"That is quite all right, Zebulla," Wendell said.

Zebulla's cracked lips pulled back into a smile at his comment. Her eye fell on Gilbert. "For some reason, when the Baron started his Conversions, he began in the town of Briar, causing the souls to stay and haunt the town. When I and all of the others were converted, we were kept in a prison, raised from youth until we turned of age to be made into robots."

"I read about that. I've also been told of the lottery they have."

"Lottery?"

"Yep," Rodney explained, "if you are chosen early, like when you are twenty-five, you are converted right then, instead of having to wait until you are thirty."

"Interesting. The Baron has pushed his horror further, weeding out humanity more and more. Back when I and my people were converted, we all waited until the age of thirty and were chopped up by an axe-wielding squad."

"Did he not keep your, uh, skin to cover the stuff inside of a robot?" Gilbert asked.

"At that time, he was still experimenting. Since you are just a boy, I would rather not bother you with the gory details of the Baron's cruelty that I and my people endured. The graveyard above us," she pointed, "was already full of cadavers in the ground. When the Baron stole our souls from our original bodies, he brought them here, in this Sector, and buried them."

"How do you bury a soul? It isn't solid, right?"

"True. What the Baron did was use a machine to withdraw the soul from the body and place it in a small canister made of an odd metal. With ours, he somehow compressed us all together in a larger canister and buried us. Eventually the canister corroded and we all escaped, slipping into these corpses. Since Heaven has cut us off, we really had no other place to go."

"Could you have stayed as ghosts?"

"I suppose we could have. I guess we all missed having flesh to live in. Even if it is decayed."

"Of what little I have already seen, the Baron seems to be collecting enemies."

"He has more than you could ever know, Gilbert. Stay as far away from him as you can."

"We'll try," Wendell answered for Gilbert. "Zebulla, have you found out if there is a doorway to another Sector? We need to find a way to return Gilbert and Bobby to their own world."

"Oh. Forgive me, Wendell, I had forgotten that the two boys were not from here and needed to return to their own land. My mind just isn't what it used to be. I have already sent out someone to find the doorway, and it has been found."

"Great! Where is it?"

"I will have someone lead you there. It will be a short walk."

"Was it the one we saw earlier? Before we were brought down here?" Bobby asked.

"No. It is a good thing you four did not open that door and walk through. You would only find a pitch black void into nothing. It leads nowhere."

"Oh."

"Thank you, Zebulla, your hospitality has been warming," Wendell said.

Gilbert was thankful, but he thought if it had been warmer the smell would have been worse!

"Zot," Zebulla said to the zombie who brought Wendell and Bobby in the room, "take these people to the doorway." Speaking to the four, she said, "Take care, all of you. I hope you find what you seek."

"Thank you," Gilbert replied.

"Again, thanks, Zebulla," Wendell said. "Okay guys, let's get. We need to find the right doorway home for you two." He pointed to Gilbert and Bobby.

Following the zombie, the quartet exited through the door that connected to the surface, leaving behind the Land of the Dead.

* * * *

The moon still hung full and vigorous above, splashing the ground silver. Zeb led them to a door that stood beside a huge, massive old tree. The quartet expressed their thanks to him; then he smiled and returned to Zebulla.

"That door looks almost like the one me and Rodney went through before we met you, Wendell," Gilbert said.

"It looks a bit complex with the lights blinking off and on," Wendell said.

"The last one had red lights above. This one has green ones."

"I hope we do better figuring out the combination, this time," Rodney said. "We were almost killed!"

"Was that before you met Wendell?" Bobby asked.

"Yep," Rodney replied and stepped up to the keypad and started punching in a combination of buttons.

"Yeah," Gilbert said, turning to Bobby, "we almost died. A robot was after us."

"Wow! That is wild!"

"I wouldn't want that to happen again."

"Mundo-exacto!"

Gilbert opened his mouth to say something else, but stopped. "What did you say?"

"Exacto-mundo, dude!" Bobby said.

"I could have sworn you said it backwards."

"Backwards?"

"Yeah. Must have heard you wrong."

"Could be."

Wendell stood by Rodney, watching his fingers work, trying to figure out the combination so the doors would open.

"Probably should have asked Zeb if he knew the right numbers to push," Gilbert said.

Wendell glanced over his shoulder. "If he did, I think he would have opened it for us."

"Yeah, you're right."

After a few minutes, Rodney gave up. "I've pushed a lot of buttons, and nothing has happened."

"Let me try," Gilbert said, stepping up to the pad. A few more minutes passed by, and he gave up. He kicked the door, frustrated. "I don't understand that!" Gazing up at the green lights, Gilbert saw that they winked on and off, as if they were laughing at his failure.

Wendell took a stab at it, failed miserably. "There's got to be a way through."

"Maybe we can smash the keypad!" Rodney said.

"No. Then it'll never open."

"Sometimes. I've seen that on movies," Gilbert said, rubbing his nose.

"Movies?" Wendell cocked his head to the side.

"Movies?" Rodney followed suit.

"Yeah. Oh. Wait. You two don't know about TV and programs and cartoons, do you? I sort of told you about them, Wendell."

"I remember. Did you say Car-tunes?" Wendell asked.

"It's car*toons*. They're like, er, uh…" He looked at Bobby for help explaining it, and all he did was shrug his shoulders. "Guess I'll just have to think about how to explain it."

Wendell smiled. "That's fine. Right now our first priority is figuring out the code on that keypad. I don't know what other numbers to come up with. And, really, we have no idea if it's one number, two, three, or four numbers in a row to punch in."

Gilbert nodded, agreeing with him.

"Let me try," Bobby said and stepped in front of the pad. He kept his back toward them so the others could not really see which numbers he was pushing, and miraculously, the doors slid open.

Gilbert and Wendell looked at each other; a shocked expression surged across both of their faces.

"How'd you do that?" Rodney asked.

"I don't know. Beginners luck, I guess," Bobby replied with a shrug.

Inside, over the threshold of the doorway, lay a dirt path through a wooded area. A cool breeze blew from within and caressed each of their faces.

"Well. Guess we'd better move. Never know, the door might shut on us," Wendell said and stepped through.

Rodney, Gilbert and Bobby followed, and as soon as they stepped in, the scenery rippled and changed before their eyes. And the doorway disappeared.

"What the heck is going on?" Gilbert's eyes were wide.

"I don't know," Wendell replied.

The dirt path and the forest had been replaced with a city. A bright sun shone down upon a decrepit scene. Buildings climbed the sky, some with huge holes in the sides where one could look directly inside. Some were missing rooftops as if a massive claw had ripped them away. Streets were littered with old vehicles.

As Gilbert stood with the others on the cracked pavement running like veins beneath human flesh, he could see inside the vehicles and noticed clothed figures sitting behind the steering wheels.

The figures were skeletons.

"Now where do we go? Find another door?" Gilbert snapped.

"Calm down, it'll be okay. We'll get you two back some-how," Wendell said, though his tone was not very confident. Even he had to scratch his head at this. He wished he knew the answer to their troubles. "Let's start searching for a way out of here."

Gilbert, distraught, nodded.

"This place looks creepy," Rodney said, gazing at the bro-ken windows in the many shops that lined the street. Manne-quins stood erect inside. A few were missing heads, hands and other body parts.

Passing vehicles, Gilbert now snatched a better look at the boney hands of the skeletons gripping the steering wheels while their mouths gaped open in silent screams. They had not a bit of flesh, only ragged clothes that draped over their frames like burial shrouds.

A slight chill rubbed its invisible finger along Gilbert's spine.

"I've never seen any place like this," Wendell said.

"Kinda reminds us of our world," Bobby said. "Just not torn to pieces. Right, Gilbert?"

Gilbert nodded.

"It's like a futuristic Briar," Wendell said, his eyes gazing intently, back and forth. "What are those things called?"

"They're cars," Gilbert explained. "Think of it like this: Horse-drawn carriages that don't need the horses because the carriage has a motor."

"Really?" Wendell was intrigued.

"Yep. No kiddin'."

They came to a cross street and noticed that the streets appeared to be endless. More buildings. More vehicles. More skeletons.

"Where to?" Rodney asked.

"I don't know," Wendell said.

Gilbert caught movement behind one of the cars. It looked like the face of a dog. "Hey! Looks like a dog over there!"

Wendell saw it and started to walk toward it.

"Where are you going?" Gilbert asked.

"I'll be fine," he said over his shoulder, "we're on the same side. Both of us bleed canine blood."

"But what about us?" Rodney said, taking a step backward.

"We'll be okay. Don't worry, you all. I'm sure the dog is more terrified of us than we are of him."

"I hope you're right, Wendell."

A low growl surfaced from the dog.

"It's okay, boy, no one is gonna hurt you," Wendell said to the dog. "We're the good guys." He wasn't ten feet from the dog when it rose on two feet. Wendell stopped. His mouth hung ajar.

"Everything okay?" Bobby asked.

"Stay back! All of you!" Wendell shouted.

"I thought you said we'd be okay!" Gilbert said.

The figure that stood before Wendell was far from bleeding canine blood inside its veins. A dog skin was draped over the small body of a naked child. Holes were torn out so two blue eyes could peek out. Both dried and wet blood matted up in the fur.

The child took a run and launched itself at Wendell, knocking him down to the pavement.

"Oh no!" Gilbert shouted and ran forward.

Rodney came next; Bobby brought up the rear.

Wendell was able to push the child off of him. The small body rolled across the ground, jumped back up on two feet, and snarled. When it noticed Gilbert and his reinforcements, the child took off down an alley.

"Where's it going?" Gilbert cried.

Slow to get up, Wendell rose, placing a hand on his neck, looked at his palm. "Don't know. Kid tried to bite me, though!"

"What do we do now?" Bobby asked.

"I think we need to leave that savage child alone and find a way out," Wendell said.

"Sounds good to me," Rodney said.

"So, which way are we going to go?" Bobby asked.

Wendell sighed deeply. "I guess going in one direction would be good as any. Let's go down this street," he pointed, "and not in the same direction as that dog-child."

Wendell took the lead again with the rest in tow. They traveled down five blocks of ruin, observing the dead inside their metal coffins. Gilbert noticed a small boney hand sticking out from under an overturned car, holding plastic keys on a keychain. He stepped over to it, bent down to look at it closer.

A shadow fell over Gilbert. "Is that a kid's?"

"Yeah, Rodney."

"Oh, wow."

"It's sad, man."

"We need to keep moving. The sun isn't helping us much," Wendell said, wiping sweat from his forehead with his hand.

"I know," Bobby said, repeating Wendell's actions.

A little farther, passing a wooden sign that looked as if something had chewed a piece out of it, they heard a howl. Wendell whipped his head over his shoulder. Another howl came, squirming out from in between two buildings.

"That doesn't sound good," Gilbert said.

"Uh. If you think the sound is bad, look ahead of us," Bobby said, pointing to the pack of naked children wearing the skins of dogs who stood about a hundred-feet away.

"What do we do now, Wendell?" Rodney said, his face clouded with fear.

"Let's backtrack," Wendell replied and glanced over his shoulder where there was an open space tucked in between two buildings. "C'mon, guys. Follow me!"

The quartet took off, and the shadows of the decrepit buildings crawled over them as they entered. Each of them had to hurry through, nearly turning their bodies sideways. Tall grass brushed their legs. The aroma of decay hit their noses like a balled-up fist.

Behind them, the dog children took chase, howling.

An alley came next, and the four sprinted down it only to

be met by five of the savages running forward to meet them, head on.

The group slid to a stop, switched directions.

More of the children appeared, draped in decayed dog skin.

Wendell saw a ladder that was attached to a building and began to climb. Gilbert came up second, grabbing the rungs, while Rodney came up third. When Bobby brought up the rear and reached them, two hands covered in dried blood reached out and grabbed him and pulled him off the ladder.

Gilbert heard Bobby cry out and looked down. "Bobby! Wendell, they've got him!"

"We'll get him back, Gilbert!" Wendell shouted, still clambering upwards. But at the back of his mind, he wasn't sure how.

Below, the alley filled up with more children and Bobby was hauled backwards, lifted over the heads of the children, out of sight.

Wendell reached the top and scurried across the flat roof. Gilbert followed close behind. Before Rodney grabbed the last rung on the ladder, two hands broke through a window and grabbed him, pulling him into the lurking darkness.

Not noticing this, a few seconds later, Gilbert glanced over his shoulder. "Where's Rodney?"

"He's not back there?" Wendell shouted.

"No!"

They came to the end of the roof. A metal plank was set up between the rooftops.

"We have to cross *that?*"

"It's our only way, Gilbert."

As soon as Wendell placed his foot on the plank, a swarm of dog children climbed onto the roof and ran after them, howling at the top of their lungs. Wendell grabbed Gilbert and placed him in front of him and said, "Go! Now!"

"But what abou—"

"I'll try and fight them off. Get across that thing!"

"But, Wen—"

"GO!"

Gilbert went, stepping one foot on the plank. At first it bent with his weight, but held fast. Slowly, cautiously, he took another step. Right after his third, he made the mistake of looking down, and the horror of falling into an alley rushed up at him.

He licked his lips. Swallowed hard. He faced forward and did not look back when Wendell cried out.

As his foot stepped on the other rooftop, he looked back and saw Wendell struggling under a pile of dog flesh and children. Small bodies lay to the left and to the right, where they had been knocked backward.

They were rising back up for another attack.

Something crackled behind Gilbert. Turning around only gave him an eyeful of six dog-children ready to pounce on him.

Gilbert stumbled back, found the plank.

The children moved forward.

The idea of being caught by these savages did not give

him good visions. He wondered if the dried blood they wore was dog or human.

Wendell was being dragged away, still trying to fight.

Gilbert took another step. The children snarled and growled and gazed at him as if he were a piece of meat. The word "Gilbert-Q" came crashing into his mind. Like barbeque. And he did not like it.

On the other rooftop, with Wendell now missing from the scene, a gang of dog-children appeared.

Gilbert was trapped in the middle. He had no idea what to do. The ground below really didn't look any better, either.

Twenty feet downward was a balcony. It could be his only hope if he could jump down on it.

Or his demise if he fell and snapped his leg in three places.

Standing there, he made the choice to try. On both sides of the plank, the savages converged at the same time.

And Gilbert leaped.

As he fell, the wind's fingers slid under his shirt, through his hair. His lower body went one way, his upper went another, and he knew that if he didn't adjust quickly he would probably break his neck. He wouldn't have to worry about anything else being broken under his skin. Death would pluck him out of existence.

Trying to adjust himself, waving his arms, moving his legs, did no good, and his fall became longer than it should have. But as soon as he was about to land, he disappeared. Winked out of the air like a light bulb.

Standing on the ground, gazing upward, was a figure dressed in black. He turned around and walked away.

When a shadow of a building fell over him, he too, winked out. Whispered away like a ghost.

* * * *

Sounds. Voices.

Gilbert stirred awake, raising his eyelids as his vision was filled with a bleach-white room. He sat on a floor made of tiles. Rubbing his face with his hand, he got up. Dizziness slammed into him, and he stumbled as the room shifted. In slow motion everything returned to normal. Or so it seemed.

A small door slid open in the wall, and two red eyes peeked out. "CONVICT 890-676-GLBRT. YOU ARE DE-TAINED UNTIL FURTHER REVIEW. DO NOT AT-TEMPT TO ESCAPE. YOU ARE UNDER ARREST FOR TRESPASSING; ESCAPING FROM PRISON; RESISTING ARREST; HARBORING A FUGITIVE; ACCOMPANYING A FUGITIVE; BREAKING LAW 128-9 IN THE BOOK OF BLOTH STATING THAT NO ONE IS ALLOWED TO MOVE FROM ONE SECTOR TO ANOTHER WITHOUT PERMISSION; ASSOCIATING WITH A LYCAN-THROPE; ASSOCIATING WITH A CANNIBAL; ASSO-CIATING WITH ONE WHOM IS A VAMPIRE; ASSOCI-ATING WITH A GHOST." The voice paused. "CONVICT 890-GLBRT, DO YOU UNDERSTAND THESE CHARGES?"

Gilbert did not reply. He was too overwhelmed by everything the voice accused him of.

"CONVICT 890-GLBRT, DO YOU UNDERSTAND THESE CHARGES?"

An invisible, thick blanket of worry hung off Gilbert's shoulders. He felt that this could very well be the end of the line for him. "How can I be charged with all of those things you said? I'm just a kid," he pleaded.

"CONVICT 890-GLBRT, DO YOU UNDERSTAND THESE CHARGES?"

Gazing at the white walls, Gilbert felt as if they were pressing inwards. "I want to go back home!"

"CONVICT 890-GLBRT, DO YOU UNDER—"

"Let me out of here, WHOEVER YOU ARE!" he screamed.

"CONVICT 890-GLBRT, DO YOU UNDERSTAND THESE CH—"

Gilbert covered his face with both hands, and his next words were muffled when he asked: "Where're my friends?"

"PLEASE ANSWER THE QUESTION."

Gilbert dropped his hands. His eyes watered. "ANSWER MINE!"

"PLEASE ANSWER THE QUESTION FOR THE RE-CORD. CONVICT 890-GLBRT, DO YOU UNDERSTAND THESE CHARGES?"

"NO! No! NOOOOO! I DO NOT UNDERSTAND THE CHARGES!"

The floor shifted five feet from Gilbert. A tile slid over, and a pedestal with a large book on top of it shot upwards. *The Book of Bloth.*

"PLEASE READ THE FINE PRINT. HERE IS A WRIT-TEN EXPLANATION OF YOUR CHARGES." The book flipped open by itself and turned to the page it desired. Gilbert stood over it, trying to read it. His mind couldn't adjust to the way the book's text was written. It was like trying to read Greek. The words were big and confusing for an eleven-year-old boy to comprehend.

After a few minutes, the voice returned. "BY READING HAVE YOU UNDERSTOOD THE TERMS IMPLE-MENTED FOR YOUR CONVICTION?"

"No."

"THAT IS THE BEST EXPLANATION THAT I CAN GIVE. NOW. PLEASE GO WITH THE TWO GUARDS ON YOUR LEFT."

Gilbert hadn't even noticed the two armed guards standing there in front of an open doorway in the white wall. It was as if they'd appeared out of thin air, and it startled him.

"Come with us, Convict 890-Glbrt," one of the guards said.

Gilbert obeyed and walked down a long hallway with one guard in front, one behind, reminding him of when he was sandwiched between the two sinister ghosts back at the abandoned house. He was led down to the end of the hallway and through another door, where he was told to sit in a chair in the middle of another bleach-white room with four walls. No sooner than his butt hit the seat, the wall in front of him became a large screen with a familiar face staring at him.

"Hello, Gilbert."

"Stephen?" The flashback of Stephen's trickery, leading Gilbert into that large field that started all of this terror, came crashing down like a huge sledgehammer.

"I see you have a good memory."

"You tricked me!"

"Nah. Not little 'ol me?" He looped his thumbs in the suspenders of his bib overalls. "I would do no such thing, Gilbert."

"You led me into that field! Now I'm a prisoner!"

"I merely asked if you wanted to find Bobby. You could have just walked out of the door to that house, and all of this would have never happened. You could have been back at home in front of the television watching reruns of *The Twilight Zone*. That is your favorite show, is it not?"

"How did you know about that?" Gilbert was taken aback.

"I also know that," the skin on his face quivered, "you recognize this face, too."

"Tilbit?"

Tilbit's feature giggled. "No. I'm not really Tilbit. He is no longer flesh and blood. His Conversion has been started."

"Then who the heck are you?"

"Why, Gilbert, I'll kindly show you." He licked his lips, and his entire face swelled up. When it deflated, it became the face of the Baron. The exact one from the pictures Gilbert had seen in the hallway, depicting the horrible camera poses by the guillotine and the electric chair. Each one where the Baron had cheesed for the camera. Even the one where he was strangling a corpse.

And smiling, smiling, smiling.

"The Baron!"

"In person!" He threw his head back and guffawed. His Adam's apple bobbed up and down. "You know," he said, calming down, "you have been such a hard catch. I would have thought Gerald would be able to hold onto you until my guards came to get you, but you were gone. Thanks to that miserable brother of his, Wendell."

Gilbert gave him a cold look.

"Then, there was the Carnival of the Bizarre. I didn't know that you were going to try and save Rodney." He shook his head. "You shouldn't hang around a nasty cannibal. They are disgusting creatures."

"Not Rodney! He's my friend!"

"So he is. But a child like yourself should not hang with such trash."

"Take that back!"

"I will not, and you, young man, are in no position to make demands here. You are under my roof. I make the laws!"

"What about Bobby? What have you done with him and the others?"

"At this minute Wendell and Rodney are getting ready for their Conversions."

"You are going to turn them into robots?"

"Yes."

"That isn't right!"

"They broke my laws, Gilbert. Now they'll pay for it."

A thought slipped under Gilbert's skull. "I thought that children were not converted into robots! They have to grow up first!"

"Well. Guess this time I'm making an exception."

"You are a terrible guy!" Gilbert snapped.

"Been called worse, young man."

If steam could have poured out of Gilbert's ears, it would have. He was furious!

"Well." He cleared his throat. "I need to oversee the Conversions and make sure that they go well." He walked out of the picture.

Gilbert's face flushed. He started pacing back and forth, his hands balled into fists, hanging down at his sides. He needed to find a way to get out of the room. Somehow. Anyhow! He wanted to go home. He wanted to find his best buddy and go home. But he also wanted to help Wendell and Rodney. The thought of those two converted into robots chilled him.

He gazed around the room, looking closely at one wall, the next, then the next, and finally looked directly into the eyes of the Baron on the large screen.

He stumbled backward.

The Baron guffawed again. "Gilbert, you are one of kind. Most people accept their fate, since it is an everyday thing here on Hearth. But I can see that anger you have. It's useful, you know? Especially in a situation such as this. Are you up for a game?"

Gilbert looked into the Baron's eyes, trying to see of it could only be a trick. He couldn't tell. "What do I win?" he asked.

"Why, you will win your friends back. I my even release all three to you."

"How do I know you will?"

"You don't. You'll just have to take my word for it. Anyway, what have you got to lose? If you don't make it, well," he shrugged, "that would be the end of you. A food thing to be well aware of is that you will not have to endure the horrible Conversions. And, Gilbert," he said with a huge smile, "they are painful."

Gilbert only stood there, appalled.

"So. Do you take the chance to save yourself and your friends from the dreaded Conversions?" He held out one hand, palm up. "Or not?" He pointed to a wall with the other hand, and a screen on Gilbert's right showed an overview of a sleeping Wendell, a sleeping Rodney and a sleeping Bobby lying on three different surgical tables. Leather straps crossed over their legs and arms. Large blades and huge saws sat on metal carts at each bedside.

With the fear of imagining those sharp tools being used to cut open all of his friend's flesh, Gilbert faced the Baron's grinning face and said, "I'll take the chance."

"Thought you would, young man." He chuckled. "A door will slide open on your left. Walk through it. Instructions for the game will be self-explanatory. Even a monkey can understand it."

The door slid open, and darkness peeked out.

"If I get through this, you'll release my friends?"

"That is what I said."

Gilbert sprinted into the doorway and was engulfed in darkness.

* * * *

Lights slowly lit up overhead, one by one, running a pathway along the ceiling down a long hallway and escaping around the corner. Behind Gilbert was a solid wall. The door that he walked through appeared to not exist. On his left-hand side stood a chrome podium with a blue screen on it. He looked down at it, read:

RULES OF THE LABYRINTH

DO NOT STUMBLE
DO NOT FALL
DO NOT FEAR
OR YOU WILL DIE LIKE ALL

Some encouragement, Gilbert thought. He feared what the Baron's maze had in store for him. He was all alone. No Wendell. No Rodney. No Bobby. Nobody to help him.

But this was the only way to save his friends from that terrible Baron!

So, without further ado, he began walking down the hallway and took a left where the pathway eventually ended in a T. Gilbert wondered which direction he should go.

There was a low hum rising from somewhere that lasted no more than a minute, until it died off.

Gilbert went right. He followed along as the path led him through a couple of turns until he came to a wooden door. Behind it he heard a moan. He stepped back a few steps while the moan grew louder, as something pressed on the other side of the door. To Gilbert, it sounded like someone was in pain.

He backed away.

No sooner had he done so than something slammed against the door, twisting and turning the doorknob. Gilbert stumbled backward and watched as a dark red liquid oozed out of the bottom, crawling toward his shoes.

Gilbert bolted back the other way. When he reached the T again he heard the door splinter and break, giving a reverberation that ping-ponged down the hall.

The moan grew louder and slithered through the air.

Gilbert sprinted. He took one path and it dead ended. He had to turn around and go back the way he came, hearing the moan seeming to close in, as he wound around two turns until arriving in front of yet another door.

This entire world is made up of doors, doors, and more doors! Gilbert thought.

There was a difference this time, however: unlike the other doors, this one was Alice-in-Wonderland small. Glancing over his shoulder, he did not see any sign of anything coming after him. Nor did he hear the dreaded moan anymore.

The hum returned a bit louder, and this time it sounded like some sort of machinery running. It rose, fell, died away.

Gazing at the small door, he wondered if it would be

possible to fit through it. He bent down on his knees and reached out for the doorknob, then paused, waiting for a moan or some type of sound to reach his ears.

But nothing came.

He grabbed hold of the doorknob, turned it, peeked inside. Another hallway looked back at him. He slid through without getting stuck and stood up.

The small door slowly creaked shut on its own and latched.

The path ended at another T, and there was a door on each side of him. A skull hung on one. At first, Gilbert thought it was human, but further observation brought the possibility that it was vampire. Two long fangs hung below its nose, with one of the sharp ends broken off. And the long shape of the face appeared to be that of a bat.

On the other door something pulsated, leaking blood, pooling into the floor. A closer inspection brought a chilling discovery to Gilbert. He remembered watching enough horror flicks to know that this thing on the door was a brain. Underneath its wet crimson shade it looked pinkish in color. Veins ran through it, crisscrossing back and forth, nearly resembling a spider's web.

The organ continued to pulsate and drip blood.

Gilbert drew away from it, not wanting to picture what could possibly be lurking behind it.

Suddenly the brain wiggled, fell, and bounced off the floor, leaving wet red marks behind where it hit. From deep inside the core there was an odd tearing sound. Six different small spots sliced themselves open, and slim, robotic spider legs pushed through with a wet sound. The skin on the front of the brain peeled back, and a single cyclopean eye filled with a blue computer screen blinked at Gilbert.

Wasting no time, Gilbert took off.

Behind him he could hear the *tick-tick-tick-tick-tick* of the spider legs.

Around a corner was a long hallway stretching so far that Gilbert could see no end. But he didn't stop. He ran as fast as he could. There were no doors on either side of him, only blank white walls.

Tick-tick-tick-tick-tick.

Halfway down the corridor Gilbert felt his body thrust forward, as if a huge vacuum was in play. When it stopped, he nearly stumbled and fell.

On his right-hand side he saw the brain shoot forward— or get sucked forward – ahead of him and roll across the floor like a basketball with a sped-up version of its eerie *tick-tick-tick-tick*ing sound.

The brain stopped and stood on its spider legs.

Gilbert was running too fast to stop and leapt over the beast. Two robotic legs reached out and brushed his leg, and he felt the steel crease his bare skin. Gilbert hated the feel of it, and when he hit the floor he ran even faster.

Without warning he was thrust forward again, and this time he lost his balance and slid. Rising up, he saw the brain shoot forward and land directly beside him, then roll away like a bowling ball.

He was up quick. He made it past the creature as a door stood waiting for his arrival. He reached it, grabbed hold of the doorknob, wrenched it open, and ran inside, slamming the door behind him.

The brain hit the door, rocking it in its frame. There was a pause—the door rocked again. Gilbert figured the creature was getting a running start and slamming into it.

Gilbert saw a metal latch that he could slide over, barricading the door. He slid it over.

The brain did not stop its attack, pounding on the outside.

The hum came back. It was very loud, seeming to make his bones vibrate beneath his skin. He stood in a small space that overlooked a wide room full of machinery. Bright lights warmed large rectangular pieces of steel with hoses running out of them. Blinking red and blue and green lights winked on and off.

A glass door stood a few feet away, and he opened it and stepped through it as the sound blasted him. The noise of the cogs, belts, pistons and pumps was entirely too loud, causing Gilbert to hold both hands over his ears.

A yellow-painted, ladder-shaped walkway under his feet led five feet forward and took a sharp turn. Gilbert followed it. As he did he viewed a long room, huge, filled with more rectangular machinery. Each machine leaned backwards, a glass dome bulging outward, while a figure lay inside each one.

Gilbert passed by the first one, noticing that there was a woman inside of it. Her hair was long and red and her figure

was slim. A dress covered her frame, catching the blood splatter from the workings of three robotic claws.

The first one peeled the flesh on her face off.

The second one dug out her eyes.

The third one sheared off the front of the skull.

A fourth claw appeared and dug into the face, worming
its way into the chest cavity, making the body twitch and
opening it up for the robotic parts to be placed inside.

Gilbert looked away. The sight was beyond horrifying.
He moved to the next, managed to watch the finishing
touches of three claws attaching a blank piece of oval-shaped
steel over the head of a man. Fingers on one of the hands
curled into the palm, lightly brushing it, and back out.

All around Gilbert humans were going through Conversions. He did not want to witness any more of it and shielded
his eyes away from the horror—until he noticed one familiar
figure.

Then another.

And another.

Gilbert backed away, horrified.

In a row behind the bulged-out glass were Wendell,
Rodney and Bobby. They were no longer laid out on the surgical tables. Gilbert wondered if they had been here the
whole time.

The claws were working on Wendell and Rodney. But
not on Bobby. His friend looked like he was in a slumber. An
idea slipped under Gilbert's skull, and he acted on it.

Studying the machine, he wondered if there was a switch

or some sort of button he could push to release his friend. Scanning the huge object, trying to keep one hand over one ear to block the persistent noise, he saw a large red button with the word OPEN over it.

Taking a chance, he pushed it.

The glass lifted up, and there was Bobby.

Lucky him! Gilbert wondered why it had been too easy.

He climbed up on the machine and shook Bobby. After a minute or so he opened his eyes. Gilbert unstrapped him, got back down, and waved him down. Slowly, Bobby climbed out. While he did, Gilbert noticed a glass door tucked in between two of the machines on the other side.

He pointed to it and the boys headed straight for it, opened it, and slipped inside, leaving the hideous noise behind.

"Gilbert!" Bobby smiled. "Good to see you! Hey, I think I know the way outta here! Follow me!"

Gilbert did not argue and trailed behind. He so wished not to leave his newly found friends, Wendell and Rodney, to their Conversion fate. He wanted to help them, to try and save them from the dreaded Baron, but he knew at this point he could not.

The very next door they came to was metal. Bobby hit a few buttons on a keypad on the right-hand side. When it opened, familiar scenery filled Gilbert's eyes.

They were back in the old abandoned house by the river in Deputy Point. Back home!

The boys stood in the hallway, the door they had exited

through, now wooden, latched shut behind them.

"Let's get home, Gilbert! We're back!" Bobby's excitement was contagious, giving Gilbert the same sickness.

Both boys raced home and were beat, huffing, trying to catch a breath as they walked down their street. Bobby said goodbye to Gilbert, telling him he needed to let his parents know that he was okay. He'd be over to his house to help explain what had happened to Gilbert's mom and dad.

The boys knew that their parents had to be worried sick!

Gilbert watched Bobby slip inside his house and shut the door. He wished that he could have saved Rodney and Wendell, but he couldn't. He hated the fact that he'd had to leave them behind! His friends had risked their lives to save him.

Gilbert wished there was some way to repay them.

Hearing a lawnmower start up, he looked over and saw Mr. Houchen across the street beginning to mow his lawn.

Gilbert waited for him to turn off the mower and look in his direction. When he did, he waved. The mower stopped. Mr. Houchen stood there for a split second staring at Gilbert before returning the gesture, as if he were having trouble remembering what to do.

A second later a smile spread under the old man's nose, and it didn't look friendly.

Gilbert felt a chill. What was up with that?

He entered his house and didn't see his mom and dad.

"Mom? Dad? You here?"

No response came.

"Mom?"

Gilbert had seen their cars in the driveway. Maybe they were out back. Dad could be in the garage. No sooner had he placed his hand on the back door than he heard the television down in the basement switch on. He descended the stairs, and there were his mom and dad sitting on the couch, both heads turned toward the screen, their hands lying in their lap.

"Mom? Dad?" he asked.

Together, at the same time, his mother and father swiveled their head in his direction. He had to step back. Their eyes had been replaced with blue computer screens.

"Why, Gilbert," his mother said, "where have you been? We've been worried sick!"

"Did you go into that house, son?" his father asked with a twitch of his head. "We told you to never go in there."

Gilbert's lips quivered.

His father stood up. "Oh, well. What's done is done." Twitch. "Can't fix it, can we, dear?"

Mom's face looked up at Dad, and one of the blue screens in her eyes rolled. "No. Not now." She reached for the remote, pointed it at the television, hit a button.

"Hello there, Gilbert." The Baron's face filled the screen. "Welcome to Sector One. I see you finally made it home. It is what you wanted, correct?"

Gilbert could only nod in agreement.

"See, I have won. I always win. And you'll need to meet your new best friend. Look behind you."

Gilbert pivoted and saw Bobby standing there beaming.

Blue screens were in his eye sockets. Had he not noticed that before? How could he have missed that? *Wait. Earlier, Bobby kept his face away from me while he was speaking and—*

"Hey there, Gilbert! Told ya I'd come back so I could explain things!" the new Bobby said with a smile.

"Meet my newest creation, Gilbert," the Baron's voice spoke. "This is unlike a Mini, like your good friends Vinnie, Twitch and Munch! I merely had them built. But Bobby? Ha! He was gutted like a pig and reborn! My very first child robot!" He guffawed. "Rodney is going to be the next!"

Terror washed over Gilbert, cascading down to his feet. His knees buckled, and he stumbled backward into a recliner.

Heavy steps fell on the basement stairs.

"Now, Gilbert," the Baron said, "my associate is going to escort you back to the same room you came from. I believe you have met him before. He'll escort you back to the Conversion Room first. Then, after you've become a robot, you'll be destined to work for him forever, being his servant."

Gerald stood there at the bottom of the steps, grinning. "Thought my brother would be able to rescue you from me, huh?"

Gilbert did not respond.

"Thought you'd pull the wool over Gerald's eyes, huh? Not this time, boy. You just wait till I get you back my cabin in Sector Four. Lots of work to be done!" He gazed at Gilbert's mom and dad. "This boy has to learn respect." He pointed his finger at Gilbert. "He has to learn not to disobey!"

"Quite right, Gerald," Father said with another twitch.

"Most certainly, Gerald," Mom agreed.

"Exacto-mundo!" Bobby said.

If Gerald's glaring eyes could have bored a hole in Gilbert, they would have right then. "After you, boy, time's a wastin'." Gerald stepped to the side.

Gilbert walked slowly up the steps. Terror filled up his body. A large lump lay in his throat. He didn't want to be turned into a robot or go back to Gerald's cabin! This was insane!

Out in the sunlight, Gilbert was told to slip inside the passenger seat of a black Cadillac. Gerald slipped behind the steering wheel, still grinning, and started the engine. They drove off as the reflection of the town of Deputy Point washed over the car's windows. People walked down sidewalks and worked in their yards and washed their cars.

Gilbert wondered if they were all robots. Had he caused all of this? Deep in his gut, he felt as if he would never see his world ever again.

The Cadillac hung a right, heading straight for the old, abandoned house.

"Wait till I get you back to Sector Four, Gilbert," Gerald said, gazing in the rearview mirror, lighting up a cigar. "I'm gonna put your butt to work. You'll have oozing blisters on both your hands and feet!" He guffawed.

The stench of the cigar repulsed Gilbert. He felt as if he'd hurl chunks.

Gerald took a right and passed a few more houses. On one lawn, two children were tossing a ball to each other, laughing, while their parents sat on the porch.

If those kids only knew about the Baron, Gilbert thought, knowing that there was nothing he could do. He was helpless, like a fly caught in a spider's web.

"Yeah, you'll only get to eat once a day and get three whole glasses of water," Gerald added, puffing away. "You'll wish the Baron Converted you, boy." Gerald looked over his shoulder. "You'll wish you had all those cogs and belts and—*ugh!*"

Everything happened in the blink of an eye.

A large truck came out of nowhere and plowed into the Cadillac, sending it for a spin, cutting off Gerald's words. The side windows shattered, and Gilbert shielded his face just in time as glass shards sliced into the side of his hand. If he hadn't done so, he would have lost an eye. And his seatbelt locked up and pressed against his body, nearly pushing the wind out of him.

He caught a glimpse of Gerald, who wasn't in a seatbelt, being knocked into the side door, his hands trying to grab for a purchase with no result. Before the car stopped spinning, Gerald had been thrown out of the car and was lying on the pavement with blood pooling around his head.

Trying to take a breath, Gilbert felt pain wrack his body. His head swam. His bones hurt. He wondered if he had cracked a rib. He tried to hit the button to release the seat-belt, which it did not do. Tugging on it did nothing.

Then, footsteps.

Gilbert turned his head just in time to see a familiar face

with green eyes attached to a tall, stocky frame wrench open the passenger door and ask: "Are you okay, Gilbert?" Wendell's voice was frantic. "Are you okay?"

"Y-Yeah. I'm...I'm fine."

"Let's get you out of there. Darnit! I didn't mean for this to happen this bad!" With ease Wendell used both hands to break the seatbelt's connection, releasing it, relieving the pressure on Gilbert, and helped him out of the vehicle.

"Thanks, Wendell."

"Are you okay, then?" Wendell bent down, studying the boy from head to toe.

"Yeah, I'll be fine." Gilbert noticed the body of Gerald. "But your brother isn't going to be. I think he might be dead."

Wendell walked over, looked down at the sprawled out figure, nodded, and said, "He's gone. Suits him right, even though I know it's bad to say. The guy was always mean."

Gilbert leaned on the car, a bit dazed.

Wendell came back over. "Should have gotten somebody to show me how to drive that...uh...that machine there." He pointed, trying to find the right word.

Gilbert asked, "Truck?"

"Yeah. That's what that guy told me when he let me drive it."

Gilbert observed the dealer tags on the license plate and the price of the truck hanging in the side window. "You drove a brand new truck?"

"Yes. That was the only thing I saw when I came through the doorway. It was sitting there with a lot of others."

"Wendell, those vehicles aren't for use in crashing into a car and saving someone."

Wendell shrugged his shoulder and said, "Worked, didn't it?"

Gilbert cracked a smile. "Yeah, it did. I'm not going to complain about it."

"We need to go," Wendell said. "I think we'll have company soon, if we don't. Can you walk on your own?"

"Sure. I'm fine."

The lycanthrope started off.

A horrid thought crashed into Gilbert's skull, and he took five steps before stopping.

Wendell had about fifteen feet on Gilbert when he noticed the boy still standing there. He turned around and said, "C'mon! We need to go!"

"Wendell, I saw you in the Conversion chamber. Those robotic claws were working on you."

"Well," Wendell explained, "they didn't damage my head. I woke up, somehow, from whatever they injected me with, and the only thing converted was my left arm. See?" Gilbert hadn't noticed before, but his friend wore a glove. When he took it off, his hand was robotic. "I can make it work, for whatever reason." He opened and closed it. "They were getting ready to split my head open next. I broke out of the chamber before they attempted to."

"Weird."

"Now, c'mon. We have got to go!"

And off they sprinted down a street.

* * * *

Night came, blanketing Deputy Point, and the two found themselves hiding out in an abandoned warehouse, not very far from the old house. Windows ran along one wall, and Wendell stood to the side, looking out, careful not to be seen.

"Where can we go, Wendell, where the Baron can't find us?" Gilbert asked, sitting only a few feet from the lycanthrope, on a stack of pallets.

Not turning around to face Gilbert, Wendell said, "We'll have to find another door to another world. That's our only chance, Gilbert."

"Where would it be? Back at the old house?"

"I don't think so. When I came through I didn't arrive in the house. I arrived standing just outside the door of a closed-up hardware store."

"That's weird." Gilbert paused. "Did you follow that doorway with the keypad?"

"Yeah."

"So did Bobby and I. We ended up right back in the house."

"Well, obviously, Bobby tricked you."

Saddened, Gilbert replied with, "I know," and a long sigh after. "Can't believe the Baron did that. Took my best friend."

"The Baron will do everything in his power to corrupt life. Whether the plan is to destroy the race of humans or werewolves or vampires." Wendell walked over, and his stocky frame shadowed Gilbert. "Don't worry, you'll be safe with me. I'll find a good place for you to go."

"What about you?"

"Me?"

"What if they catch you? Then what?"

"If they get me, Gilbert, then you run and keep running. Don't let that demented guy's robots get you."

Gilbert knew that was easier said than done.

"All right," Wendell said. "The plan will be to camp out here for the night until morning. Maybe we can find a door to another world. One where the Baron doesn't rule."

"I thought he ruled everywhere."

"Well, I've heard stories about other places on the planet and, together, we are going to find out if they're true."

Gilbert was confused. He was under the impression that they were all in a world of Sectors.

"Try and get some rest. You'll need it tomorrow."

Gilbert got up and found an old mattress that smelled bad, but he didn't care. As tired as he was, he lay down, and before he realized it, sleep overcame him.

Right before his eyes shut, he watched as Wendell continued to stand guard, gazing out of the window.

* * * *

The sun woke Gilbert up. He rose, stretched, and immediately saw Wendell still standing in the same spot as before. He asked, "Did you see anything last night?"

"No. Everything's been just fine," Wendell responded.

"That's good." Gilbert walked over to him. "So, where do you suppose we need to go to hide?"

"Right here should be fine. We don't need to go anywhere else." The tone in Wendell's voice had changed. It was flat.

Gilbert cocked his head to the side and frowned. "I thought you said we needed to find somewhere else to hide. This place wasn't safe."

"Sure it is, Gilbert. Don't you worry. I'll take care of you." He turned his head, gazed down at Gilbert, with blue screens inside of his eye sockets. "All you need to do is go back over there and rest. Everything will work out for the best."

Shocked, Gilbert backed away. "You can't be one of them! You said so yourself! You showed me your arm!"

"There is something they call microscopic spiders that can build from the interior out," the robotic Wendell explained. "This arm of mine," he raised it, "was infested with the creatures. The old Wendell did not know. He was oblivious to what had happened to him. Sure, he escaped the Conversions, but they hand-delivered the rest of the process—so to speak—packed inside this arm waiting for the right moment to strike."

Gilbert felt the life drain out of him. What could he do now?

"Now, if you would be so kind in accompanying me back to the old house where we will be transported to the Sectors and to the Baron, you will be placed back in prison and will work as needed." The robotic Wendell stretched out his hand. "Once you are a robot, Gilbert, everything is better.

No worries, my friend, no worries at all." A smile stretched across his face.

"No!" Gilbert shouted and ran off, heading for the only door.

"STOP! CONVICT 890-GLBRT, YOU MUST STOP!"

Gilbert heard a voice unlike Wendell's. Something mechanical shifted. Parts moved, adjusted, fabric ripped and tore. As much as he did not want to, as his hand fell on the door handle, giving it a slight push down to release the latch for it to open, he looked over his shoulder.

And freaked.

Standing there was a new kind of Wendell: taller, stockier, transformed into a robotic werewolf. Chrome, razor-sharp teeth lined the inside of his jaws. Huge claws sparkled in the sunlight. His shredded clothes hung off his frame, and inside his eye sockets bright green glowed, spearing Gilbert.

"COME WITH ME, CONVICT 890-GLBRT. YOU MUST BE DETAINED AND TAKEN BACK TO THE BARON," the voice from Wendell's huge maw said.

Gilbert turned the latch and bolted out of the door and ran as fast as his legs would carry him.

The robot crashed through the door and took chase.

Quickly, Gilbert ran towards downtown, curving around a building. A long street full of shops and a few restaurants filled his view. Parked cars sat along the curbs. Only a few people strolled down the sidewalk.

He had run about a block and a half when he had to stop to take a breath. Glancing over his shoulder, thinking he would hear the pounding of the robotic beast closing in, he saw no sign of Wendell. He wondered where the beast had gone. Was he hiding? Waiting for the right time to snatch him?

Gilbert rubbed a hand across his face and sighed. Everything had backfired. He'd thought Bobby was okay, only to find out he had been Converted, like his parents. Now, Wendell. Gilbert was at a complete loss about what to do. He felt like giving up.

"Hello there, Gilbert."

That voice.

"Hello, Gilbert." Laughter followed.

Turning around, Gilbert hadn't realized where he was standing: directly in front of a repair shop. Computer monitors and televisions sat in the window. There was even a mascot-like figure made out of stovepipe with a small television for its head. Rabbit ears, an antenna, added to the touch.

The Baron's face looked out of about five screens, laughing. "Thought you could escape me, boy? There is nowhere you can go in the Sectors! You will be caught and brought to me! And your punishment will be the CONVERSIONS!"

Gilbert backed away, watching as the demented man threw back his head and guffawed.

He rocketed down the sidewalk and was about to cross the street when he noticed two figures slip out of a floral shop. Each held a bouquet of roses in its hand. Each gazed at him with blue-screened eyes.

Gilbert backtracked, heading for the old house. He wondered if there was an actual door inside that place that would deliver him into another world, away from this horror.

Behind him, he heard running footsteps.

A large crowd had formed, and on each side of him more people poured out of doors. Oddly, each one held roses.

Gilbert nearly ran into one guy who darted out in front of him, trying to grab him with one hand. "We are all coming to your funeral, Gilbert. We are all bringing flowers…"

The words chilled Gilbert to the bone. But he did not stop as he rounded another corner, now having the old house in view.

"CONVICT 890-GLBRT, YOUR ARE TO BE DE-TAINED AND BROUGHT BACK WITH ME," Wendell's voice echoed down the street. The mechanical beast material-ized out of an alley, caught up, and ran alongside of Gilbert, trying to swipe him with its huge claws.

Gilbert ducked, feeling the wind off the claw, and ran as fast as he could to the house. He hoped there was refuge there. He had no choice.

The crowd grew larger and larger behind him, gaining. Wendell led them on, while each figure still grasped their beautiful flowers.

Gilbert ran up to the porch and in no time was inside the house. A musty smell smacked him in the face, and he sneezed. Closing the door, looking around, he was almost sure that those two ghosts—Phillip and Margret—would be waiting for him.

But there was no sign of them.

Hurriedly, he took the steps by twos and was on the first floor in no time. Doors lined the hallway; some stood open, some did not. He tried every one, only to find an empty space reflecting back at him.

Downstairs, the door crashed open.

"Come on out, Gilbert. We know you are in here," a woman's voice shouted.

Gilbert ran up to the second floor and saw that each of the doors was closed.

"COME OUT, CONVICT 890-GLBRT. GIVE YOUR-SELF UP."

Frantic, Gilbert tried to open each door, found them unlocked, and with the memory of all the horrendous things that he remembered seeing before—when the evil duo showed them off—he closed his eyes before opening a few of the doors. Relieved after finding the rooms vacant, he decided to go to the third and last floor of the house.

Footsteps climbed the stairs.

The third floor was small, with less rooms. Gilbert began trying each door. When his hand fell on the last door, his hope was crushed.

The crowd had found him. Wendell was in the lead.

"COME WITH US." The robotic Wendell was not asking.

"Get away from me!"

"Child," a woman stepped away from the lycanthrope, "it is all better here. The world through our eyes is a better place. You must understand. There is peace and harmony."

She stretched out her hand that held the roses. "This will mark your burial. Your last life as a human. We have all come to give our respects to the dead."

Chilled, Gilbert grabbed hold of the doorknob and twisted it.

"No! Stop!" a man shouted as the conglomerate of people all moved forward as one. "Do not go in there!"

The door swung wide, and the view of a dreary sky and a land full of woods filled Gilbert's vision. The wind was cold, and not very far away were headstones sticking out of the ground.

"DO NOT ENTER THERE! DO NOT ENTER THERE! THAT IS OFF LIMITS!" the robotic Wendell screamed.

Gilbert didn't listen. He had finally found a doorway into another world, a dimension, or wherever this was. As quickly as he could, he stepped inside and slammed the door behind him.

* * * *

The large crowd gathered around the door, not even touching the doorknob.

Displayed on the door was a large pentagram.

Now the entire robotic crowd and the robotic werewolf were well aware that their target had escaped.

When the news reached the Baron, he would become very angry and perhaps, just perhaps, dismantle them all.

ABOUT THE AUTHOR

Married to a woman who keeps him chained up in a room so he won't try to escape and turn his fiction into a reality, Brick Marlin silently resides in the Ohio Valley.

*For your reading pleasure, we invite
you to visit our web bookstore*

WHISKEY CREEK PRESS

www.whiskeycreekpress.com